SCREAM

SCREAM FOR SARAH

Veronica Heley

CHIVERS

British Library Cataloguing in Publication Data available

This Large Print edition published by AudioGO Ltd, Bath, 2013.
Published by arrangement with the Author

U.K. Hardcover   ISBN   978 1 4713 1997 6
U.K. Softcover   ISBN   978 1 4713 1998 3

Printed and bound in Great Britain by
MPG Books Group Limited

CHAPTER ONE

Everything was all right until the tramp arrived. Or was it? Had things started to go wrong before that, with Toby's arrival?

I am not quite sure how it was that Toby got himself invited to Elm Tree House in the first place. Apparently I'd asked him at the office party, although I couldn't remember having done so. It wasn't as if I knew him well, although I had been out with him a couple of times in a crowd for a drink after office hours, and I had danced a lot with him on the night of the party. I wouldn't have thought he was serious about me, but he must have been to have travelled some eighty miles from London to visit me. I knew he'd had to take special leave to come, and it wasn't even as if I were there on holiday, but to clear the place of my grandmother's belongings.

I suppose I was flattered, for at the age of twenty six I, Sarah Long, felt I was in no position to turn a prospective husband from the door. That is, assuming that Toby was a prospective husband, and he had certainly been acting like one.

Elm Tree House was the grandiose name given to the pair of ancient cottages which my grandfather had knocked into one dwelling and modernised some twenty years ago. There was the stump of an elm tree at the far end of the garden, which was large enough to occupy my grandfather almost exclusively in the years of his retirement. It was the garden which had killed him in the end, since he had insisted on digging a trench for his sweet peas while recovering from a bout of bronchitis. My grandmother could never bear the scent of the flowers afterwards.

And now my grandmother had also died, and hens scratched wild in the cobbled yard and neglected garden.

There was a Family Council after her funeral, and it was decided that as I was the only unmarried member of the family, and as I had inherited my grandmother's jewellery, I should clear Elm Tree House of her belongings, prior to its sale. I didn't fancy the task, but I had been my grandparents' favourite, and I owed them something, because I had spent nearly all my holidays with them when I was a child. My father and mother have never been able to have a discussion about anything without it developing into an argument, and in my youth I had deliberately chosen to spend my free time out of reach of their clacking tongues. This time my parents were actually at one on the subject; they would pay my air fare to go abroad on holiday, if I would first clear out Elm Tree House. It was high summer, and I was feeling jaded; I agreed, and wangled an extra week's sympathy

2

leave from the office. I didn't think I'd done too badly out of the deal, until Toby came to join me.

I hadn't really expected him to come. He'd said he would muck out the hen-house for me—a job which I detested—but I couldn't imagine him doing it. 'For you, I would!' he'd said. I disliked Granny's hens, and one of my tasks that week was to be to sell them to the neighbouring farmer who had been keeping an eye on them since her death.

I got away on Wednesday night, and spent all day working at the house on Thursday before Toby arrived, bearing a ready-cooked meal for supper. I blessed him for that, and we opened some of Granny's home-made wine to go with it. Yet I was uneasy; I hadn't any good clothes with me, and I didn't feel I showed to advantage in a sweater and jeans. Then Toby took my car out and dented the wing; I still couldn't understand why he hadn't taken his own car when he went to get some cigarettes after supper; he said it had been giving him trouble, but it started all right when he drove it into the garage on Friday morning. We use a solidly-built converted stable as a garage, but there is only room for one car in it, and I didn't see why his car should be housed there, instead of my Mini.

Another thing; he kept on saying how perfect the house was, but he didn't seem interested in the, building itself; he wanted to

3

know how often tradesmen came down the long muddy lane from the road, and how far away we were from our nearest neighbours. It did cross my mind to wonder if he wanted to be sure no-one would hear me if I screamed when he made advances to me, but of course that was nonsense. In the first place, I'd have liked him to make advances to me, because I felt it was about time I lost my virginity, and in the second place I don't consider myself the screaming type. The fighting type, yes; I've brought my knee up once or twice when men have got too fresh with me, but screams are definitely out. They are a waste of time and energy. Besides, I didn't make a habit of getting into situations where I needed to scream for help.

Why, then, did I feel so uneasy?

Toby was Mr. Good Manners himself on Friday morning. He helped me wash up after breakfast, and promised to muck out and feed the hens for me, after he'd had just one more cup of coffee. That was nice of him. Of course by that time in the morning I'd already let the hens out and fed them, but he could clean the henhouse for me with pleasure!

He was charming. He was everything that I'd always wanted in a man. He called me pretty names, such as Butterfly and Quicksilver, and said he'd always liked his women to look fragile. He measured my height against his, and tucked me under his

4

shoulder to give me a hug. I had daydreamed of his kissing me, but when he did, I pushed him away. I said it was too early in the day for canoodling, and that I had come down to the house to work, and not to play. I could have hit myself afterwards, for instead of looking hurt, he shrugged and asked for another cup of coffee.

Fool! I told myself, but I didn't try to kiss and make up. There was plenty of time for that, I argued, as I went upstairs to make the beds. Elm Tree House boasted two bedrooms, one big double bedroom at the head of the stairs, in which Toby had slept the night before, and a smaller single room leading off that. It wasn't an ideal arrangement, especially since the bathroom also led off the main bedroom, and there was no access to the bathroom from the smaller bedroom without going through the master bedroom. Last night I had slept in the small bedroom, as I had done as a child, and wondered if Toby would try the door. He hadn't. I suppose I was disappointed about that, too.

A dealer in antiques had been to see me the previous afternoon, and had taken away an old desk and a set of dining-room chairs, together with the best of the china and a brass lamp. He said the rest was junk, but that he'd give me a price for it when I was ready to leave. In the meantime I had to clear cupboards, a chest of drawers, cabinets and shelves of knicknacks, ancient bottles of medicine, and a mountain of old clothes. Also the kitchen. I started on the wardrobe, carrying piles of old clothes down to the yard to burn. They smelt fusty and after a couple of trips I felt dirty and tired. The morning sun promised a hot day.

'And is my little kitten in a better temper now?' Toby asked, beaming at me over a cup of coffee.

'Worse!' I said shortly.

'Have a drink,' he suggested. He was intrigued by the shelf of home-made wines in the kitchen. I declined on the grounds that it was too early in the day for me to drink anything but coffee.

'You haven't a cigarette?' he asked.

'You know I don't smoke. Anyway, I thought you went for some last night.'

'Yes, but . . . I couldn't get my favourite brand. I went from one pub to the next, but no luck. I told you.'

'The Swan down the road usually stocks the lot. You must have been drunk . . .'

'You know I wasn't. I was sober when I came back, wasn't I?'

'After one and a half hours! All that time to look for cigarettes . . . Come off it! And that edgy, with it!'

'I don't know what you mean!'

'Bad-tempered. On edge. You might have been apologetic about it . . .'

'About what? The dent in the car? Well, I

6

am sorry about it, but I couldn't help myself. I just didn't notice that gate post at the end of the lane . . .'

'It's painted white, and has a reflector on it. Besides, you didn't make that dent by bumping into a gate post. You can see it must have been made by something . . . well, not something with a hard edge to it, like a gate post.'

'What, then?'

I shrugged. We were sitting in the big living-room of the cottage, with the front door open onto the yard. Clucking hens bustled between us and my little Mini, sitting full in the sun.

'Another thing,' I said. 'Why should your car be parked under cover, and mine be left outside?'

I stumped out to inspect the damage, intending to change the cars over. Toby followed me, trying to jolly me back into a good humour.

'Look at it!' I shrieked. I was buying the Mini on the Never-Never, and it was the pride and joy of my heart. The nearside wing was badly dented, and this in turn was affecting the cant of the headlight.

'I said I was sorry! Come on, now. I'm concluding a very big business deal at the moment. In a few days we'll go back to Town together and I'll buy you a brand-new Mini, instead of this second-hand heap. Then you can have this one broken up for scrap, which is about all it's good for, if you ask me.'

7

'You can't be serious!'

It seemed he was. Charming, generous Toby. Only I was no grateful yes-woman, ready to cast myself into his arms and tell him that I'd love to have him take care of everything for me. As my mother has always said, I have no tact at all where men are concerned. Besides, I loved my Mini, second-hand or no.

Aware that I was once more jettisoning my chances of marriage, I refused his offer. One part of me was always wanting to swoon at a man's feet, but the other part wouldn't allow me to do so. Regretfully, I decided I'd made a mistake in inviting Toby down, and equally regretfully I saw it would be a bad idea to allow him to stay on during the coming week. Now we both knew I wasn't going to hop into bed with him, the situation would be embarrassing.

'Just get it repaired,' I said. 'And as for staying on here, don't you think you might find it boring . . .?'

At that moment the tramp pushed open the garage door and fell into the yard.

I screamed.

I didn't actually leap for Toby's arms but he got them round me somehow.

'Christ Almighty!' breathed Toby. 'Where did that come from?'

That uncurled itself and staggered to its feet. One dirty claw was extended towards us while he shielded his eyes from the sun with the other. He was filthy; mud-caked and bloodied. His boots were enormous and without laces. His coat and trousers hung on him in concertina folds, patched and torn, allowing glimpses of brown skin here and there. He might be any age from twenty to sixty, a stunted, stick-like, mop-headed monstrosity.

I've always been terrified of tramps. I clung to Toby and begged him to protect me. 'Don't let him come near me!'

'Of course—I'll drive him away!' But he took his time about releasing himself.

The tramp's eye alighted on my car. To tell the truth, he acted as if he were uncertain where he was. He stared at my car as if he were seeing a ghost. From the back he looked even odder than from the front; he clutched at his trousers with one hand, so as to prevent them from falling down.

'The road's that way,' said Toby, advancing on him.

The tramp turned his head. He opened his mouth to speak, but no sound came. His eyes swivelled, looking for an escape route. He looked like a trapped animal, awaiting the coup de grâce.

'Wait a minute!' said Toby, in a hard, surprised voice.

The tramp began to run, lurching and slipping in his ludicrous boots. Toby overtook him without effort, and tried to stop him by grasping at his coat. The tramp lashed out

9

with claw and boot, but only succeeded in infuriating his pursuer.

'Like that, eh?' Toby laughed, and disregarding the tramp's feeble attempt to dodge, dropped him flat on the cobblestones.

The tramp moved feebly and then lapsed into unconsciousness. The hens squawked and flapped away from us, disturbed.

'Why did you do that?' I cried.

'He was here to steal, wasn't he?'

Toby checked that the tramp was out for the count, and then went to the garage to fetch the chain and padlock which had been used years ago to restrain my grandfather's dog when she was on heat. He dragged the tramp, legs trailing, to where an iron boot-scraper had been sunk into the flagstones at the side of the front door. He clipped the chain round the man's ankle, and secured it to the scraper.

'Better check he didn't steal anything last night,' said Toby, going through the tramp's pockets. I looked away. Much as I hated tramps, I didn't like to see a man treated like a parcel of fish, to be trussed up and turned over and prodded like that. Toby was so big and the tramp was so small that my sympathies began, little by little, to alter direction. Now that he couldn't harm me, I began to see that the tramp was such a poor specimen of a man that if he had molested me, I would have been able to deal with him.

'That's enough!' I said, as Toby wrenched

10

off the tramp's remaining boot, and stripped off his jacket. His torso was bare and brown, splotched with blood and mud. His right arm and the back of his leg were badly bruised. There was a pale, broad band of skin around his left wrist which argued the absence of a wrist-watch.

Toby agreed that it was indeed enough, but he stood looking down at the man for a long moment before he joined me indoors.

'He came to steal eggs I expect,' I said. 'The sooner I can get rid of those hens the better. If you'd mucked out the hen-house as you promised, you would have found him earlier, because the tools are in the garage.'

'I wish I had,' said Toby. He helped himself to a beer and sat down, drying his forehead with the back of his hand.

I was trembling, too. I don't like violence, and I don't like tramps. One had followed me on a country walk once, and I'd never forgotten him; a great shambling brute of a man with a vacant expression on his face. My adult mind knew that such men were more to be pitied than feared, but childhood fears die hard. I got out the telephone directory and looked up the number of the local police station, thinking that it was a blessing that Granny had insisted on having the phone put in.

'What are you doing?'

'Ringing the police. They'll deal with him.'

'Lock him up? No, don't!' He broke the connection. 'I've a better idea.'

I had never liked him so much as when he explained how he felt about locking up the unfortunates of this world. Toby believed that he, and other educated people ought to try to help those who were unable to help themselves, and not just hand them over to the authorities to be locked up. He said we ought to try to help them, instead.

'But it was you who knocked him out when he was trying to run away!'

'My first instinct was to protect you, and make sure he hadn't stolen anything. Then I got to thinking that I'd acted dead against my principles, and that if the tramp got into the garage for shelter, or needed to steal eggs because he was hungry, then we ought to help him. We have so much, and he has so little. He had no money on him, you see. Not a penny.'

'The police could give him a handout, couldn't they? They could give him better clothes, and a chit to the Labour Exchange . . .'

'They'd probably jail him first for trespass and stealing eggs! You don't want to send a man to jail, do you?'

'N-no . . .'

'Then let's keep him for a few days. We'll give him some work to do, and let him doss down in the garage at night. Then when he's earned some money, we can send him on his

12

way with a few pounds so that he can get a fresh start. Without money he can't buy new clothes or obtain accommodation, and without new clothes he can't apply for a job. He's in a vicious circle of poverty, and he can't break out of it on his own. We could help him to do so.'

'But I don't like tramps, and although I know it's silly, I'd be afraid to have him around me.'

'I'll cope. You won't have to talk to him or do anything but tell me what jobs you want him to do.'

He looked excited and pleased. I couldn't find it in me to refuse him his wish to do good, so I agreed. I got out the cutlery box and all the materials for cleaning silver, and directed Toby to set up a bench and table outside so that the tramp could do the job in the open air. I didn't want him in the cottage. Toby gave me a lingering kiss to show his approval and I melted. I knew that just because a man was big it didn't mean that you could look up to him morally, but in this case I thought I was on to a good thing, for Toby had proved himself big in every way.

I started to make a shopping list while Toby instructed the tramp in his duties. Presently I heard Toby's voice raised in anger, and then the sound of a slap. I didn't like violence, and I didn't really think Toby needed to use any on that shrimp of a man.

'He can't talk!' said Toby, returning. 'He's dumb. Not deaf, but definitely dumb. I can't get a word out of him. Either that knock I gave him earlier, or some illness perhaps . . . For all I know he's been like it from birth. He doesn't seem to know his name, or where he came from or where he was going to. You can see his mind goes blank when he tries to remember!' The tramp's plight seemed to amuse Toby.

'Can he understand you? Does he know what he's supposed to be doing?'

'He understood that all right. Where are you going?'

'Shopping.'

'I'll do it.'

'But I don't want to be left here alone with a nameless tramp. What would I call him?'

'Hob the Hobo, perhaps? That would be a good name for him. He'll not bother you. He's chained up, remember, and he understands what he's to do. I'll take the Mini to a garage and see if I can get the dent knocked out, and do your shopping on the way back. You can get on with your clearing out in peace and quiet, and tonight we'll dress ourselves up and go out. I see there's a Jazz Festival on somewhere nearby. Do you fancy it?'

I'd seen the posters, too. 'I wouldn't mind,' I said, 'Even though I'd have to go as I am.'

Toby went off in my Mini, and I found myself work to do inside the cottage. I didn't want to pass the tramp, so I made excuses not

14

to go outside. At twelve I made myself some sandwiches and a cup of coffee. It was a baking hot day, and even inside the thick walls of the old cottage, the air was thick and warm. I had an argument with myself about feeding the tramp, and then took him out a sandwich and a mug of water on a tray.

He had finished cleaning the silver, which was gleaming in the sun. Now he was resting, lying at full length on the bench, his bruised and bloodied feet towards me. The chain round his ankle allowed him just enough leeway to get both feet onto the bench. I didn't like to look at him too closely, but I couldn't avoid seeing his feet.

I pushed the tray of food onto the table, and he sat up, slowly. I stepped back, to be out of his reach, although the table was between us, and he could not possibly have hurt me from where he sat. His eyes fixed on the tray I had brought him; Toby was right, and the tramp was hungry. But when I reached for the knife box and silver cleaning things, he raised a hand to stop me. I dropped the tray in fright. He tried to smile, to reassure me. He pointed to the mug of water and made washing motions over his face and hands. He wanted water to wash himself in.

This evidence of civilised behaviour reassured me. I promised to fetch some for him, and this time he let me remove the silver. I brought him a bowl of warm water, soap and a rag of a towel. He had drunk half the mug of water by that time, but not touched the food. He thanked me with a dignified bow that should have been ludicrous, but wasn't. He had dark brown curls all over his head, and although his hair was tangled and thick with muddy patches at the moment, it might once have been attractive. I have always wished that my hair were curly; I won't go through all the rigmarole of perms and weekly sessions at the hairdressers, so instead I keep my hair cut short and neat, close to my head.

I watched him from the doorway. He luxuriated in the water. I could hear his intake of breath as he touched a bruise, but he didn't miss any. In silence I fetched him a refill of water, and he got to work on the rest of himself. He was wearing nothing but a reasonably clean pair of blue pants; I wondered where he'd pinched them, for they actually fitted.

'More water?' I asked, when he reached his feet. He nodded, his eyes wary, but not unintelligent. It was difficult to tell how old he was, even now. A beard that had once been trimmed to a reasonable shape covered the lower part of his face, but his teeth were good. His nose was no splodge, though it did widen at the tip. His forehead was square under a loose mop of hair without a thread of grey in it, but the crowsfeet around his eyes marked him as a man past his twenties.

16

His feet were a mess, and in my opinion, needed more than a wash. It was a wonder to me that he'd been able to walk on them at all. I fetched ointment, lint and bandages from Granny's medicine cupboard, and ordered him to lie flat on the bench and not move till I'd finished. He didn't stir while I washed and bound his feet, but his eyes followed my every movement, like a watchful robin. When I had finished he put both his hands together over his heart, as if he were praying, then touched them both to his forehead and spread them towards me. In thanks.

'That's all right,' I said, foolishly confused. Hob the Hobo might not be able to speak, but he could make himself understood.

From a window I watched him eat, which he did with restraint. He rinsed his fingers afterwards. I took him out a small bookcase which needed scrubbing down.

'You understand why Toby wants you to stay? You will work for us for a few days, and sleep in the garage at night? We'll pay you for what you do, and at the end of the week you can be on your way with some money in your pocket. You agree with this?'

He watched my face while I spoke, and frowned when I finished. But he nodded. I wasn't satisfied with his reaction, although I couldn't tell why.

'Can't you speak at all?' I asked.

He didn't appear to hear me, but bent down

to start work on the bookcase. I stamped my foot at him. He took no notice.

'It's for your own good,' I said, trying not to be angry with him. He didn't look up from his task, so I left him to it.

With anger came contempt for him, and I no longer avoided going into the yard because it meant passing by the bench on which he sat. He was a scruffy little man. He'd probably be no larger than me, standing up. It was a pity that all of Grandpa's clothing had been burned or given away when he died, or I could have lent the tramp something to wear. Then I laughed at myself, for Grandpa had been a six-footer, and his clothes would have drowned the tramp.

By teatime the sun had moved round from the front of the garage, and the tramp tried to move along the bench with it. The chain wouldn't allow him to move that far, and I saw him shiver.

Of course, my clothes would probably fit him all right. No, I couldn't. I could not lend him anything of mine. I'd never see it again, and . . . no, the idea was repellent.

Only he couldn't go around naked, and I had several pairs of worn jeans and some old sweaters with me. I looked over my stock and selected an ancient navy sweater and a pair of paint-stained jeans that had once belonged to one of my elder sisters and was a trifle too large for me. He took them from me

18

wonderingly, his eyes distrustful. He pulled the sweater on at once, but couldn't do anything about the jeans until Toby unlocked the chain.

And where was Toby, anyway?

He came back in the late afternoon, flushed with sun. He explained his lengthy absence by saying he'd been hanging around trying to get the garage to do something about my car. They had knocked the dent out, eventually, but the car would have to be taken back again on the morrow for the paintwork to be touched up.

Toby was both surprised and amused to see that I'd managed to transform Hob into something approaching civilised man. He chaffed me about Hob while I prepared supper, and I laughed and agreed with him that we were doing the right thing, and that I was glad, after all, that I'd not called in the police to deal with him. I said that we ought to ask Hob for his word of honour not to escape, so that we could let him off his chain. I argued that we were trying to build up Hob's self-respect once again, and that that couldn't be done while he was being treated like a bitch on heat. Toby didn't agree; he thought Hob would take off for the woods the moment we let him off the chain. We had quite an argument about it. I thought that Hob was to be trusted, I suppose because he had not turned on me when I had tried to help him. Toby said that was a poor argument, and that Hob had likely been wandering the roads for years, and had

19

forgotten anything he might once have known about gratitude or fair-dealing.

I replied that you couldn't expect him to learn how to behave like a human being once more, unless you treated him as one. Toby gave me a hug and said I was a proper little Dragonfly, wasn't I? He said he might let himself be persuaded, if I worked on him in the right way. I didn't mind. He was big and fair and strong, and I've always been attracted by men of his physical type. Mentally he had proved himself my superior, too. What more could I ask for? I did give him a kiss or two, and he gave them back to me, and we only realised how late it was when the potatoes boiled over.

While I was dishing up, Toby went out to speak to Hob. I could hear him quite clearly, putting the case to the tramp. I thought he was doing well, but unfortunately he didn't seem able to make Hob understand.

'The man's wits are wandering,' said Toby, flinging back inside, 'I can't do anything with him. We'll have to keep him on the chain, I'm afraid.'

I could see the top of Hob's curly head from the window, and I guessed he'd been able to overhear everything Toby and I had said about him.

'He seemed bright enough to me,' I said, and went outside. Hob was drooping against the wall of the cottage, his body slack. The chain still shackled his ankle, and his right leg was beginning to puff and discolour from his bruises.

'How could he have come by such injuries?'

He turned his head away from me, a stupid look on his face.

Toby came to lean in the doorway. 'A fight with another tramp, I suppose.' He was angry that his well-intentioned plan had miscarried. 'Look, Sarah, if he won't cooperate, there's nothing we can do about it except safeguard ourselves. I'm determined to keep him until he's earned himself some money. I'll do good to him in spite of himself, if necessary. I'll lock him up in the garage. He can stay there all the time from now on; he'll be out of your way there and he won't be able to make trouble for us, either.'

Hob laid his arms on the table and rested his head on them. He hadn't had anything to eat since the sandwiches I'd given him for lunch, and the aroma of the supper I had cooked must be teasing at his nostrils. Toby went indoors, probably to fetch the key to the chain. Immediately Hob's head came up. He linked his thumbs over crossed wrists and waggled them to simulate the flight of a bird. He was appealing to me. He wanted to be free. His eyes were intelligent enough, now.

'Toby!' I called. 'It's wrong to keep him against his will. Let him go?'

'No, he must work his passage, like every

21

other member of the human race,' said Toby, from within. 'This smells good, Sarah. May I start?'

'In a moment. Hob, please! Give me your word you'll not escape?' He started, and looked around. I realised he didn't know we'd re-Christened him. 'We thought we'd call you Hob, if you don't know your real name . . .?' He shook his head, his eyes blank. He didn't know his name. 'Then I'll go on calling you Hob, because you must have some sort of name, right? Why won't you give your word not to escape? You know we mean you well . . .'

His eyes slid across the yard to the Mini. He didn't seem to find the sight pleasant, but I was in no mood to be sidetracked.

'Come, now! Give me your word and I'll get Toby to take the chain off you. Then we can all have something to eat.'

He considered the offer for a while, scrutinising my face as he did so. I wasn't used to being assessed as if I were a suspect in a murder case, and yet that was the impression I got. Hob had the oddest way of reversing our roles from time to time. He nodded. He agreed. He put out his right hand, and I laid mine in his by way of sealing the pact. His hand was tough-skinned, and showed signs of manual labour—and of the fight which Toby guessed he'd been in. Properly dressed, he could pass for a sailor.

I ran to tell Toby the good news, reinforcing my plea that he should release Hob by saying that the tramp could hardly run on his injured feet. Toby was not too pleased that I had succeeded where he had failed, but produced the key and released our prisoner. There was a downstairs toilet off the kitchen, and Toby allowed Hob to use this, after first locking the back door, and pocketing the key. I set Hob a place to eat at the far end of the long table. Toby turned a shoulder on him while we had supper, but I noticed that Hob was making an inventory of the contents of the room. As I had assumed, his table manners were good, and he refused the cigarette which Toby threw him after supper. He helped me clear the table without being asked to do so, and when I showed him where everything was in the kitchen, he washed up for me.

We didn't get to the Festival after all. I suppose that our responsibility for Hob weighed on us. We turned on the ancient television, which didn't have BBC2, and listened to the news before watching a play. I fixed Hob up with a stool just inside the door, where he could watch and at the same time start to strip down an old rocking chair which my mother fancied she would like to keep. Toby made signs to me that he found Hob's presence a nuisance, but I wanted my relationship with Toby to develop slowly, so that we could get to know each other before jumping into bed, and so I ignored his hints that we should turn the tramp out of doors again.

'Pity about the Festival,' I said idly, when the news was finished. 'Could we go tomorrow?' I had been reminded about it because there had been a sizeable item on it in the news; it was being held about three miles away from us as the crow flies.

'How long would it take us to get there?'

'Not long, through the back roads. I've been to Point to Point races on the same site. It depends on the traffic how long it would take us.'

' They've got quite a crowd there. I'll see if I can get tickets tomorrow.'

Toby helped me to shut up the hens, although that was more of an excuse for him to give me a hug in the moonlight than because I needed assistance, for the hens went to roost with the dusk. He told me that my eyes were mysterious and romantic and pointed out that the moon was nearly full. Was I affected by its light? Perhaps. Toby was personable and my heart was not engaged, so I let him explore my mouth with his as much as he wished. I began to regret that I had insisted on bringing Hob into the cottage.

Toby didn't chain Hob up that night, but allowed him to sleep on the settee in the living-room. Toby locked the front door and put that key in his pocket. I checked that the windows were shut fast, although they were so small it would have been impossible for him to climb out of them. There was no lock on my bedroom door, so Toby showed me how to jam a chair under the doorknob to repel possible invaders. I made some stupid joke about my fearing him more than the tramp, but he didn't follow it up.

I slept soundly in spite of my disappointment. It was just as well that I did, seeing what was to happen the following day.

At first the morning went easily. I fed Hob and turned him out into the sun to finish stripping the chair. Toby helped and hindered me alternatively, teasing me to kiss him while I was making the beds, and making me giggle.

'Fulfil your promise,' I suggested. 'What about cleaning out the henhouse?'

He mimed horror. 'A cup of coffee?'

'Oh, you!'

I left him to his coffee, and approached the henhouse in some annoyance. Cleaning out the henhouse was a job I detested, but it had to be done. A brown paw laid itself over my head, warm to the touch. Hob pushed me gently to one side and started to clean the henhouse himself. He didn't speak, of course, and he didn't smile. He wrinkled his nose against the smell, but he persisted. I noticed he wasn't used to the job, for he took even longer over it than I would have done. But he did it, and then limped back to work on the rocking

25

chair.

Later, when I tried to shift an old mangle out of the kitchen, he materialised at my shoulder and lent his weight to mine. It was the same when I wanted to lower the washing-line; I didn't have to call Toby, for there was Hob, ready to help, very much at my service.

'You'd better watch out,' said Toby, in an edgy voice. 'Some Indian religions have it that if you save a man's life, he must serve you and yours for ever. It looks like you've won yourself a slave.'

'Nonsense!' I said. 'I didn't save his life, and it was you who didn't want him to go to jail.'

Two sets of eyes latched on to me thoughtfully. I felt embarrassed, although I couldn't see any reason why I should be.

'I didn't save your life, did I?'

It was as if a black curtain had been drawn across behind Hob's eyes. His face went slack, and he turned back to his task.

Toby's face was tight and hard.

'What is it?' I asked. 'Have I said something stupid?'

He didn't smile, or laugh, as I had thought he would, but turned away. He was fiddling with the old radio set when I went to fetch some water to wash Hob's feet.

'That doesn't work properly,' I said. 'Give it a kick, and you might raise some static, but on the other hand, you might not. I can't think why Granny and Grandpa didn't throw it away

26

and get themselves new things; they had plenty of money.'

Toby slapped the radio, but it failed to respond. He wandered around as if looking for something to do, and then leaned against the door while I attended to Hob's feet.

'It is odd,' I said, more to Toby than to Hob. 'How can his feet have come by such treatment if he had boots to wear? And look at those scratches on his legs! And what about that mark on his wrist—he must have worn a watch until quite recently.'

'Maybe he was wearing clothes which were reasonably decent until a few days ago,' hazarded Toby. 'Maybe he's a recent drop-out, which would account for his wearing a watch. I suppose he sold it to buy food, or meths. Tramps drink anything, don't they?'

'There was meths with the silver-cleaning things yesterday, but he didn't touch it.'

Hob didn't shift under my fingers, though I must have caused him pain. His face might have been chiselled from wood.

'Maybe he strayed too near the Jazz Festival,' suggested Toby. 'And if he was wearing a watch and some decent clothes, then he might have been set upon and robbed for them. Perhaps they took his own boots and left him the ones he was wearing when we found him. You can understand why, can't you? Who'd wear such monstrosities?'

'A ploughman would. But I expect you're

right.' I patted Hob's ankle as a signal that I'd finished, but he didn't thank me, as he had done yesterday.

Something was bothering me about the clothes Hob had been wearing. I picked them up from where Toby had flung them, and shook them out. A big-framed man must have worn them and the boots. No wonder poor little Hob had been mauled, for he wouldn't have stood a chance in a fight with such a big man. The suit was old, but didn't smell of tobacco or meths; it smelt of hay and damp. A prickly ear of old grass stuck to a rent in the shoulder pad. I picked it off, and rubbed it through my fingers. I tried to imagine why a man would drop out of society and couldn't. How would it feel to walk the roads by day and sleep in a ditch at night? How did a man live? Where did he find food? Obviously he had to steal to keep himself alive.

I folded up the clothes and put them on the pile of Granny's things which were to be burned, together with the boots. When I turned round, Hob was watching me, his eyes bright once again. Toby had gone into the house.

'What is it?' I asked, and for some reason I kept my voice low. He pointed to the Mini.

'Yes, it's mine.'

His eyes went opaque on me.

'Why? Why shouldn't the car be mine?'

He limped over to it, and touched the

dented wing, looking at me for an explanation. I didn't understand. If only I'd used my brains and linked it up, then and there, we could have got out before the others came.

'I bumped into the gatepost at the end of the lane,' I said, not wishing to give Toby away. Hob's face stiffened. I didn't want to forfeit his good opinion of me, so I explained.

'Toby borrowed the car the other night, and brought it back like that. It was careless of him, but he's promised to pay the repair bill.'

Hob stared at me, and then into the cottage. At that moment I realised that although he always played the idiot when Toby was around, with me he showed signs of being an intelligent and reasonable person. Holding my eye, Hob placed his bruised leg against the dented wing of the car. I didn't understand. I stood there, frowning, until Toby came out and took charge of the situation. He was jangling my car keys.

'I'm off, then,' he said. 'I don't know how long the garage will take, so expect me when you see me.'

'Could you get Hob some shoes?' A pair of Granny's bedroom slippers lay on the pile of debris. I fished them out and examined them. They might do for Hob until we could get him something better. I held them out to him, but he didn't take them.

'Not this morning,' said Toby.

'What will people think, if they see him going around like that?'

'Who's likely to see him? You said yourself no-one comes here, and that even the mail is left in that box on the road.'

'Mr. Brent, for one. You remember that I told you a neighbour had been looking after the hens for us? He said he'd drop in when he could to discuss a price. He's haymaking, so I don't know when it will be—could be any time.'

'You didn't tell me.'

'About Mr. Brent? I'm sure I did, but even if I didn't, I don't see that it makes any difference. Don't worry, no-one else is likely to come here, except the furniture dealer, and that's fixed for when I'm ready to leave.'

'It's just that I wanted this to be a nice, quiet holiday . . .' I forbore to say that he had hardly spent any time at all with me as yet. 'Well,' he said, making up his mind, 'I'll take him, then. Put those slippers on, Hob, and we'll be off.'

I hugged him, to show my pleasure. He fondled my breast, and I drew away, for I didn't like it when men made a beeline for my breasts. Hob was taking his time putting the slippers on, so Toby hauled him up and pushed him into the Mini, throwing the slippers after him. I waved them off; Hob peering through the back window at me until the car disappeared round the bend.

They must have reached the end of the lane only minutes before Mr. Brent got there, since I hardly had time to decide what task to tackle next before I heard his car arrive. I've known James Brent since I was a child and used to go with my grandmother along the footpath across the Scarecrow field and through the kissing gate to his farm in order to fetch the milk. He was a spare, well-tailored figure of a man who farmed in a big way, and was rarely seen out of immaculate riding boots, even though he didn't hunt. I liked him, and he had liked my grandparents, so that we had plenty to talk about. It was on the cards that he would put in a private offer for the house and garden, and although I couldn't talk prices with him, I did tell him that my parents would rather sell to him than put Elm Tree House on the open market.

It would suit my parents to get rid of the property quickly, even though they knew they might be able to get an inflated price from a commuter to the City; and everyone knew that Mr. Brent was anxious to acquire the house, because his head cowman's son wanted to get married and would be forced to take a job in Town if he couldn't find accommodation nearby.

We had a look at the hens, and he offered to send round a couple of lads the following morning to collect them and whatever eggs I had on hand. All I would have to do was to shut them into the henhouse tonight, and keep them shut in till his men arrived. I said I didn't care what price he gave us for the hens, so long

31

as he took them away immediately, and he laughed and said he could see I hadn't learned anything, working in the big city.

We talked of his married son, who was now farming about ten miles away, and with whom I had played as a child. His wife was now expecting her first baby. Then, inevitably, we talked of the Jazz Festival. I didn't realise how much bad feeling it had caused in the neighbourhood.

'Roads jammed for miles—people sleeping in my far barn without so much as asking—gates left open—young girls with babies clinging to them, traipsing around with no regard for their children's health—and the litter! The organisers say they're going to clear up afterwards, and no doubt they will, on the site itself. They're using Thomas's big field—you remember it?—and the paddock beyond it. He'll be all right, and he's being paid for the inconvenience, but what about my fields? And everyone else's within a range of miles? There's been a knifing already, and the wife refuses to allow the youngsters down to the village, or to go off on their own as they usually do; so they're up in arms about that! It's the drug cases that worry her, thinking that our lot might want to try some . . I don't think they would, but maybe—in a crowd—you never know. Then I've had the police around, wasting my time, about the suicide in the river down by the pollarded willows; I told them it

32

wasn't on my property—down where you used to go fishing with my lad, remember?'

'Ugh! The weeds! I remember I wanted to go swimming there once, and got belted for it.'

'Maybe he didn't know about the weeds, and went for a swim . . . full of drink or drugs, for all I know. Just left his car and his clothes . . . He'll come up when he's full of gas, maybe. Maybe not. Remember when we lost a cow down that way once? Should have got compensation for that, by rights.'

'I want to go to the Festival, though. Just to see what it's like. Toby, that's a friend of mine who's staying here for a few days . . .' Mr. Brent gave me a teasing look. 'Well, there may be nothing in it, but he's at a loose end and offered to help me clear the place out. Toby said he might take me tonight.'

'Finishes tonight. Have you got tickets? They say it's all sold out.'

I shook my head, disappointed. It didn't look as if I was going to get to the Festival, after all.

James Brent started to laugh. 'You know how much they're paying Thomas? He didn't really want to rent his field to this Festival crowd, so he asked five times what he thought they'd pay, and they agreed straight off. So he got upset because he thought he could have asked even more, and now he's got them to agree to pay him for parking, and supplying water, and laying on portable toilets and the

Lord knows what else. No haymaking this year for Thomas; he's got his men working round the clock down there, putting up fences and humping in tons of sausages and crates of soft drinks and directing parking . . . He's set to make a packet out of it, and what's more, he'll get most of his money in cash, if I know him, so he'll diddle the Income Tax people, too!'

After Mr. Brent had gone, I set to work on the linen cupboard, throwing out what couldn't be used by the family, and packing the rest away in an ancient steamer trunk. It was mid afternoon before I realised that I'd missed my lunch.

Then my Mini came down the lane, followed by a big blue van, and it was too late for that. Or for flight.

Toby was driving the Mini, and he was alone. He got out, stretched and grinned at me.

'Where's Hob?' I asked, suddenly uneasy.

Toby jerked his head at the van. 'Got a mite restless, so we locked him in there for safety.'

The van jolted to a halt, just short of the garage. It was shiny and looked new. A big, dark man in a dirty T-shirt was driving it, and there was a woman sitting beside him. They gave me the sort of glance which drivers of large cars reserve for pedestrians, and turned their attention to Toby, who was opening up the garage. He reversed his car out of the garage, and around the side of the house into

34

the garden, out of sight of anyone entering the yard.

'What's going on?' I asked.

No one took the slightest notice of me. The van was driven into the garage and parked there, also out of sight.

'What's going on?' I repeated, as Toby came round the side of the cottage, pocketing car keys.

He didn't reply, but unlocked the back doors of the van to pull Hob down and out into the yard. Hob staggered, blinking in the strong sunlight. He located me and came to crouch at my shoulder. His hands had been tied together behind his back with string, and there was a fresh bruise on his cheek.

'That's not necessary!' I said, angrily attacking the string round his wrists. 'And you didn't buy him any shoes, I see.'

'I met these friends of mine,' said Toby smoothly. He seemed to be enjoying a joke of some kind. 'We haven't seen each other for ages, and all the time we were talking, Hob kept trying to run away, so we put him in the back of the van for safety and came back. I told my friends I was sure you would be pleased to give them a meal and to put them up for the night.'

'I don't know about that.' I jerked Hob free. He was trying to tell me something. To warn me? His eyes were eloquent, but even if he could have spoken, I couldn't have done

35

anything about it.

Toby waved the burly man forward. 'Sid, meet Sarah, who has offered to put you up tonight.'

Sid looked me over and decided I wasn't his type. That was all right with me, for he wasn't my type, either. I thought Hob kept himself cleaner than Sid, and besides, I've never liked men with beer barrels for stomachs.

'And this is Rose!'

Rose stood with one hip thrown out, model fashion, and looked me over. She was wearing a strapless, bra-less top and sleek slacks. It was the sort of outfit which looked marvellous if you had the equipment to fill it—which she had. She was tall—a good five foot nine in her heavy heels, and she wore the longest pair of false eyelashes that I've ever seen. She was also wearing an expensive perfume. A more unlikely companion for Sid you could hardly imagine. I looked at her and then at Toby, and I knew without having to have it spelled out for me that Rose was Toby's girl, and that their relationship was not that of 'Old' Friends, but very much of the present.

Rose didn't say she was pleased to meet me, because she wasn't. She looked around her and shrugged, as if to say that it was beyond her to comment on the uncivilised surroundings to which Toby had brought her.

My eyes switched to Toby, who was watching us both. He was smiling.

'I don't understand,' I said, and heard my voice ring flat in the sunny yard. Hob sighed and dropped his head into his hands.

'I don't understand!' My voice rose. Everyone but me seemed to be in on the secret, and I didn't like it.

Sid cleared his throat. I waited for him to spit, but he didn't. He jerked his head towards me, but addressed himself to Toby. 'Didn't you tell her, then?'

'No. I haven't told her anything.'

Sid twisted his eyebrows. He was not used to thinking quickly. 'But you said . . .'

'I said there'd be someone to drive the van, I know. But Reggie couldn't make it. I phoned him last night, and again this morning but he's still tied up with the bogies watching his every move on account of that big job he pulled last month. He can't slip away without bringing them up here after him.'

The bogies. That was a cant term for police, wasn't it? A big job—a robbery? Drive the van—for what purpose? I opened my mouth to demand explanations, and Toby got in first.

'You don't understand!' He was mocking me. 'How very dumb you are. The Festival, nitwit! With oodles and oodles of lovely money rolling in. The turnstile money, the rent for the field, and the rights for parking and toilets and food. All the money's been kept in a safe supplied by Old Farmer Thomas and guarded night and day by his trusty men. He doesn't

37

like banks, he doesn't. He's afraid the Inland Revenue will spirit all his profits away if he checks the money into a bank. He wants his cut in cash, doesn't he—the greedy old man! He made it a condition of allowing the Festival Committee to use his site, that he should have his cut in cash on the last day of the Festival. The tickets are sold out, and they know precisely how much money they have coming in. At this very minute Old Farmer Thomas is sitting in front of the safe counting out his share, closely watched by his band of men, and by the members of the Committee. And early this evening one of the better-known Security Firms is going to send a van to the site to collect the rest of the money and bank it. Only we're going to nip in first and collect the money before the real Security Firm gets a chance to lay their hands on it. A good scheme, eh?'

Rose spoke from behind me. 'She's hardly tall enough.' I jumped, and sidestepped Hob to face her. She was frowning, but delicately, so as not to disturb her paint job.

'Why shouldn't the little man drive?' she asked.

'I thought of that,' said Toby. 'But he's slippery as an eel. Nearly got away from me twice today, and his feet are in such a mess I doubt if he could handle the van's pedals properly, even if we could induce him to play ball. He's hardly what you'd call responsible, either. I wouldn't put it past him to stall the van at the crucial moment, just for the hell of it. No, Sarah will have to drive for us.'

'I'll see you damned first!' I shook with rage and fear. Hob's hand was round my ankle, and I kicked him off. 'Get out of here! Get out, the lot of you! If you aren't off my property in five minutes, I'll call the police.'

No one moved.

I counted the odds against me, and then swung into the house. Hob followed me. He was making signs, but I was in no mood to stop and work out what he was trying to tell me. I snatched up the phone and jiggled the rest. No dialling tone. Nothing.

'The phone's dead,' said Toby, following us. Sid and Rose came in, too. Toby locked the door and put the key in his pocket; quite a collection of keys he must have on his person. 'I cut the cable myself, after you tried to make that phone call to the police about Hob yesterday. You said yourself that we're not likely to have any more visitors. We're on our own now, so let's get down to business.'

CHAPTER TWO

'Let's face it,' said Toby winningly, 'Nobody will lose a penny except the insurance companies.'

We sat around the table, the three conspirators and me. Hob sat on the floor beside me, and now and then his hand touched my ankle as if to warn me of the need for self-control.

'It's still crime,' I replied. I felt stunned. While Toby talked, I sat stiffly in my chair, trying to work out how I had got myself into this mess.

'Redistribution of wealth,' said Toby, smiling. Sid smiled, too, but Rose didn't; she watched me with wide-open, cat-like, greenish eyes.

'I'm playing Robin Hood, if you like to look at it that way.' He moved his hands expansively in the air as he talked, his shoulders wide and his expression ingenuous.

'What sort of person are you?' I wondered. 'Are you a full-time crook? No, you can't be, with a job in our firm.'

'I've not been there long, you know. Just long enough to establish a few contacts. No, I'm not a full-time crook yet, because I'm careful. I choose my jobs carefully, plan them well beforehand and spend the money a little at a time. I invest most of what I earn, because I intend to retire early. That's why I take an ordinary nine to five job every once in a while; to keep my hand in, to provide myself with a front, and a host of useful acquaintances—like yourself!'

'I never did invite you down here!'

40

'No, I could see it hadn't occurred to you to do so, but it was easy enough to persuade you into thinking that you had.'

'You were never interested in me as a person . . .'

'Not until I learned where you were intending to spend this week, when I became very, very interested. We'd been planning this job for some time, and originally I had thought we would have to travel back to London straight after the job, still in disguise. I was working on the problem of trying to find a suitable overnight stopping place where we could shed the van and our uniforms when I heard one of the girls in your office joking about your misfortune in having to postpone your holiday. She said you were so desperate for company that you'd even asked your flatmate if she could get leave to join you. It seemed providential. All I had to do at the office party was to see that you drank more than usual, and plant the idea that you'd asked me down.'

I could feel myself going scarlet with mortification. I tried to hit back.

'An amateur!' I sneered.

'A successful one. Four jobs in four years, and I clear ten thousand a year, tax free.'

'Is that before or after Rose and Sid take their cuts?'

'Before or after tax, in other words? After, of course.'

41

'And they are both amateurs, too?'

'Rose is, although Sid is what they call 'well-known to the police'. This is only the second time that Rose has worked with me, although as you've probably guessed, we've known each other socially for a long time. Sid's cousin usually works with us, but as you've heard, Reggie is tied up elsewhere at the moment, which is where you come in.'

'You are absolutely mad!'

'Far from it. I told you, I plan well, and well in advance. Rose takes the odd secretarial job through an agency when she feels like it, and early this year she found herself working on a part-time basis for the Festival Committee. She told me about it, and I saw the possibilities at once. She knows the layout of their camp, roughly how much they've taken to date by way of gate money, how much Thomas will take off that, and which Security Firm is to collect the money. Pick-up time for the money is six o'clock this evening, but we will nip in at a quarter to the hour, and scoop the lot. We have the van outside, we have the uniforms ready and paperwork sufficiently like the real thing to pass muster. All we have to do is present ourselves, and they will give us the money. Simple. After that we hare back here, divvy up, get rid of the clothes, tip the van into the river, and disappear. No one comes down here, you said so yourself. It's the perfect hideout.'

So that was why Toby had put his car first in my garage, and then parked it out of sight in the garden. He had been careful to hide even that much evidence that he was in the neighbourhood. And that was why he'd used my Mini on his trips from the cottage, and why he'd taken Hob with him that morning; not to get shoes, but to keep him out of Mr. Brent's way. Everything must appear as normal to the eyes of a casual visitor, and Hob's advent was certainly not normal. Now I knew why Toby had done no more than flirt with me. I raised my eyes to Rose's, and thought I saw a trace of pity in them. I could have screamed when I realised the extent of my folly.

'Rose must go back in half an hour or so,' said Toby, glancing at his watch. 'She has her alibi laid on; staying locally with friends tonight, and off on a Continental holiday with them tomorrow. She's been working for the Committee for months—no-one will suspect her, afterwards, but she must go back today, to collect her pay-cheque and make her farewells . . . and also to give us the final signal to go ahead.' Toby grinned at Rose, and she smiled back, pleased with him and with herself. 'Sid, you'd better get on with the van; put the insignia on the side and don't forget to attend to the windows. You'd better work in the garage, just to be on the safe side, but you can leave the doors open. Park the uniforms on the table in here when you're ready.'

43

Sid yawned, revealing bad teeth, and Toby let him out into the yard.

'Five hundred pounds,' said Toby. 'You could have a whale of a time on holiday with five hundred pounds, Sarah. All you'd have to do would be to drive the van to the site, park it in the right place, and wait while we collect the money. Then you drive it back here, help us burn the uniforms, and forget the whole thing.'

'No,' I said, as calmly as I could. 'Another thing, you have no right to keep Hob here. He can't tell anyone what's happened, so why not let him go? I can't understand why you kept him here in the first place . . .'

'I couldn't have the police butting in here just before I pulled a job, now could I?'

'But you could have let him go. Why all that talk about making him earn money for a fresh start in life?' Hob tightened his grip about my ankle. I hadn't realised he was so close to me. His hand was warm.

Toby laughed. I was beginning to dislike that short, abrupt laugh of his because it expressed not only excitement but something else as well . . . callousness, perhaps. Rose didn't seem to like his laugh, either, for she backed me up.

'Yes, Toby. Why hang on to the little man? He can't do you any harm, can he?'

'He knows too much.'

'He knows nothing!' I cried angrily, and then as I saw Toby's grin expand into another

laugh, I began at last to use my head. 'My car
. . . Hob's bruises . . . The dent in my car, and
the bruises down his leg. Toby, you borrowed
my car and were away a long time . . .'

'Telephoning Rose.'

'. . . but you didn't damage the car by
bashing into the gatepost, you damaged it by
bashing into Hob! That's why he tried to run
away when he first saw my car, and that's why
you didn't want him to go. You were afraid
that somehow or other he'd be able to tell the
police that you ran him down the other night!'

'Well . . . yes, all right. Have it your own
way. I didn't see him till I was on top of him.
He was walking on the wrong side of the road,
and I'd tossed him over the hedge before I
realised what was . . .'

'Driving too fast, you mean!'

'. . . but I stopped, and he ran away.'

'Poor Hob! You must have scared the living
daylights out of him.'

'He scared me when he materialised from
the garage, I can tell you! I thought, Christ!
Of all the bad luck, that he should pick on
that building to doss down in. Why couldn't he
have gone somewhere else?'

'I expect he saw the lights of our windows
from the road,' I explained. 'If you knocked
him down at that first bend in the road after
you leave our lane, and he got into the field
through the hedge there—or was tossed over it
by your car—then he'd see clear across to this

house. I was turning out the chest of drawers upstairs that evening while you were away, so I had the lights full on. He wasn't to know that you had come from here. How could he? So he'd come up to the house, looking for shelter. I don't how why he didn't knock us up for help. He chose the garage because it was the only building he could get into, and in the morning he heard us talking, and fell out into your arms.'

'I suppose so,' said Toby, exercising charm. 'But you'll admit we've made up for knocking him over. We've fed him and watered him, and you've even given him some of your clothes. He's only a tramp, after all.'

A sudden pressure on my ankle made me look down. Hob was staring at Toby, his expression shrewd. He had tightened his grip on my ankle involuntarily, it seemed. I considered the nature of his injuries in the light of Toby's confession, and still found myself at a loss.

'His feet,' I objected. 'Why were they in such a mess, and his hands?'

'He'd been in a fight with another tramp, or been robbed by other tramps. We agreed that,' said Toby. 'And that's enough about Hob. He's half-witted, anyone can see . . .'

'Is he?' asked Rose, She twisted her fingers in Hob's curly mop and turned his face up to the light. He relaxed and swayed with the pressure of her fingers, his face going blank.

46

'You see!' said Toby.

Rose wasn't so sure. She released Hob, and he sank to the floor, his head drooping. Was he acting? I thought he was, and Rose was undecided. We looked at each other across Hob's body, and although we didn't speak, we reached agreement on certain points. First I acknowledged that she was Toby's mistress and that I had no right to him, and second I acknowledged that I was worried about Hob, and wanted him set free. She seemed to think we had struck a bargain.

'Let him go,' she suggested. 'One less to worry about.'

'No,' said Toby. 'Not yet.' He came to stand behind Rose's chair, nuzzling her neck while his eyes searched my face for a reaction. I hope I didn't react at all, except perhaps to show something of my disgust with myself for ever having been taken in by him.

'I mustn't be too late,' said Rose, looking at her watch. 'I've got about half an hour's work to do at the site before I leave. Who's going to drive me back to where I left my car?'

'Sid will take you.' Toby went out into the yard, calling Sid's name.

I saw my opportunity, and took it. Hob couldn't run, with his feet in such a bad way. I glanced across at him, and caught his eye meaningfully. He understood. As I dived for the door, he caught Rose's knees in a bear-like hug and brought her to the ground. Then

47

I was out and running across the yard, past a startled Toby, and ponderous Sid . . . along the lane round the bend and past the stile to the Scarecrow field . . . ducking under strands of wild briar . . . stumbling along a rut . . . I ran as I had never run before. I had to reach the turn into the road before Toby caught up with me. I was a good sprinter, but not built for distance. I ran, calculating odds. If Toby got his car out to follow me, he'd have to fetch it from the back of the cottage, and perhaps reverse it, which would lose him a couple of minutes.

If I could only reach the corner of the road in time. If! I ran and caught my foot in a rut. The recent rain had softened the surface of some of the lane, but left the parts shadowed by trees as hard as ever. Pounding along, I ran with hair flopping on my forehead, and my breath hurting me . . . noises in my ears . . .

A hand on my shoulder! I ducked and dodged and ran on, to be caught such a wallop round my knees that I went headlong across the track into the hedge.

It hadn't been noises in my ears, but Toby's footsteps pounding along behind me that I'd heard.

I screamed. And again. But the breath had been half knocked out of me in my fall, and I made a feeble noise.

No one heard. How should they? The nearest house was a good mile away, and the nearest traffic a hundred yards round another bend. I could hear cars passing by, but they couldn't hear me.

I tried to kick Toby off my legs. He released me and I scrambled up, trying to dive through the hedge away from him. He clasped me round the shoulders with one arm, and with his free hand started to choke me. I clawed at his hand, and he increased the pressure. My face went hot . . . and then the sky turned black and I floated off into it.

*   *   *

I woke up to find myself lying on the floor in front of the fireplace at the cottage. My head and throat ached. I moved my tongue stiffly and tried to ease myself into a more comfortable position. Pain wrenched at my ankle and I stopped moving. Cautiously I turned my head.

Legs. Legs in slim green slacks, and legs in nicely cut trousers; Rose and Toby. Hob's legs, lying bound at the ankle, were at the far end of the room, by the staircase leading to the bedrooms. The string which bound Hob's ankles was secured to the newel-post. There was no sign of Sid.

'. . . a ruler?' That was Rose.

'Knotted rope might be better. Watch her— she's as slippery as he!'

I tried to sit up, but found my hands had been fastened behind me. A belt had been

49

buckled round my wrists. I craned my head round and identified one of my own leather belts. I gasped something about they must help me, because I was lying in such an odd position that I couldn't sit upright without assistance . .

'Or just another belt?' said Rose, ignoring my splutterings. She tugged at a hook let into the stone from which the chimney had been constructed, testing its strength. I could have told her that my grandfather used to hang his overcoat there to dry, but I didn't think she'd be interested. Toby bent over me and jerked my ankles higher into the air, tearing off my brogues and throwing them across the room. I fell flat on my back. He twisted and heaved on my legs so that I turned first on my side, and then, painfully, on my face. I tried to indicate disapproval. I tried to twist myself on to my back once more. My knees were being held up by Toby, higher than my shoulders. I managed to twist onto my side, despite his hard grip. His hands moved to my ankles, crossing them, and I thought how much crueller his hands looked than Hob's.

'Stop it!' I managed to say, but they took no notice. He bound my ankles round with a length of rope and looped the end over the hook in the chimney-breast. I floundered around like a fish caught by its tail. I didn't understand what they intended to do, but I guessed I wasn't going to like it. I began to pant with fear.

The more I tried to sit upright, the more I hurt myself, as every effort I made to sit straight sent my bare feet swinging against the rough stone of the chimney-breast.

'Sit on her shoulders, if necessary,' said Toby. Rose grounded me. I tried to heave her off. Toby helped her hold me down to the floor until she had got herself across my shoulders.

'I'll try the belt,' said Toby, in a matter-of-fact way. 'It would take too long to knot the rope, and a ruler might do too much damage. After all, we don't want to cripple her. She's got to drive the van.'

A scream burst from my dry mouth as something heavy struck the bare soles of my feet.

'There, now!' said Rose soothingly 'Only five or six . . . just to stop you running away.'

'Two!

I gurgled something and tried to buck her off me.

'Three—hold her still!'

I jerked wildly and almost unseated Rose.

'Four! Hold her still, I said!'

I couldn't bear it. I screamed again, a long wail.

I heard Rose say something to Toby as his voice triumphantly counted to five. Surely this must stop soon!

'Six!' A babel of disagreement over my head. It seemed Rose's weight had been removed, but I wasn't seeing anything too

51

clearly for tears. The room turned black at the edges and I guessed I might be going to faint. My twisted body was one scream of pain.

Then my feet fell to the floor with a thump; the jar of their fall caused pain to overtake my sense, and I hovered over the edge of consciousness. Noisy voices disputed over my head. I wished them away so that I could try to cope with my hurts in peace. They zoomed into my head, and began to make sense. Rose was telling Toby that I'd had more than enough punishment, and he was saying that I was a tough little bitch who needed breaking in.

'But she's got to drive—you said so yourself!' I heard Rose's heels slap across into the kitchen. She ran some water, and then slapped back again. Water . . . I opened my eyes, to discover that I had bitten my lip and that I was sweating. Rose lifted my head and put a cup of water to my lips. I could see her eyebrows crease in a frown as I drank. She let me go, and I collapsed back onto the floor, and closed my eyes. The voices receded.

Blessed, wonderful silence.

When I next opened my eyes, I found that the shadows had shifted on the floor around me. My eyes went to the clock on the wall, but it had stopped at five to seven, and no one had thought to wind it up again. I couldn't consult my wrist-watch, but I thought I'd slept for about an hour.

It was the clatter of crockery which had roused me. I managed to sit upright this time, and propped myself against a nearby chair. Hob had been moved. He was sitting in Grandpa's big carving chair at the head of the table; somebody had used a lot of string to make him secure, not only round his wrists and ankles but also round his shoulders. He was awake, and looking down at me with a troubled look on his face. I tried to smile at him, to show that I was still in the land of the living. His expression relaxed a fraction, then his eyes shifted in a gesture of warning as Rose marched in. She had pulled a cashmere sweater about her shoulders, but otherwise looked the same as before. She was vexed. She moved about rapidly, knocking into chairs as she set the table for a meal. She didn't lay for Hob, or for me. She didn't speak to us, and I was in no mood to speak to her.

Once she came and stood over me to inspect the soles of my feet. I didn't like to think about them. They burned. I could see that both were swollen, and that one was bleeding. I thought she might offer to bathe them for me, but she didn't. I thought that Hob would have done so, if he'd been free. His hands would be gentle, and the cold water so soothing.

I found I was crying, and ordered myself to stop. I sniffed and wiped my cheeks on my shoulders. I knew perfectly well that now was the time when I needed a clear head, and yet

53

I couldn't think straight. My mind kept on returning to the memory of Hob's torn feet, and wondering, absurdly, about them.

Rose yelled through the open door into the yard. 'Eggs and bacon, and for God's sake, hurry up!'

Toby and Sid came in, Sid grumbling that he hadn't got cloth ears, and that they'd nearly finished, for Christ's sake.

They left the door open, and I sat there, longing to be out and through it, and knowing I couldn't make it. Toby had done too good a job on my feet for me to run, or even walk, without pain.

'You'll have to wash up,' said Rose. 'I simply must be back by five at the latest, or I won't be able to give you the signal to go ahead.'

'Sid will run you to your car.'

Sid was throwing his food around. A messy eater. I averted my eyes from the sight, but was sorry when he finished.

Rose approached me, and tried to get me upright. 'Upsadaisy!' she said.

'No,' I muttered, and slid down to the floor again.

'Help me, Toby!' Between them they hauled me to my feet. I yelled as the soles of my feet touched the floor. Toby slapped me, left and right.

He let go of me, and I slumped to the floor, dragging Rose down with me. Toby kicked me. I tried to hump myself into a ball, and would not stand.

'You shouldn't have hurt her so much,' said Rose. 'She'll never do it, now.'

'She will,' said Toby. 'Just fetch the clothes, Rose, and then you can get off. You know your way back here?'

'Yes, of course. But I don't see how . . .'

'Don't worry about how. You do your part, and I'll do mine.'

'Suppose she won't help? Will you have to let Sid drive?'

'No, they expect three men; two in the van, and one driving. We can't risk not having a third. I know how to handle her.'

I sat up at that. 'Rose, don't leave me here with him. You know he means to hurt me!'

She looked upset. I think she had been shaken by the violence Toby had used on me, so perhaps she wasn't as hard as she had seemed to be.

Toby put his hand on her shoulder and whispered in her ear. I watched her face. She looked anxious at first, and then uneasy. Finally she laughed incredulously, checked Toby's face to make sure that he was serious . . . turned right round to look at Hob then back to me . . . and finally, nodded agreement.

'Rose!' I cried. But she was half-way to the door already.

'It's all right,' said Toby, falsely reassuring. 'I'm not going to hurt you any more, I promise.'

I didn't believe him. My eyes sought Hob's, and found he was watching the door. Rose came back in, bearing a pile of dark blue uniforms, helmets and goggles. She dumped them on the table, picked up her handbag, and went out without looking at me. Toby went after her. Then I heard my Mini start up, and knew Sid was taking Rose back to wherever she'd left her own car. The yard and garden behind would shortly be looking like a used car lot. The hens squawked as the Mini departed, and I wondered who would feed them that night.

Toby returned. 'Relax!' he told me, as he hauled me into a chair at the table. He didn't unbuckle my wrists, though, so I didn't take him seriously. He picked up another chair and set it beside mine. The only difference was that he'd put his chair with its back to the table, so that he could sit close to me, facing me. His thigh pressed on mine. I recoiled. He smiled, not pleasantly.

I said childishly, 'I don't like you. Go away.'

'Come now—relax! What is there to be up-tight about? You're going to earn yourself five hundred pounds this afternoon, and then go off and have a wonderful holiday. You wanted to go to Rome, didn't you? Think what a wonderful time you could have in Rome with five hundred pounds! No one will ever connect you with the robbery . . .'

'Fingerprints!' I said. 'No alibi. They'll

search everywhere, locally.'

'No fingerprints, because you'll wear gloves, of course. No one will recognise you, either, because you will wear a man's uniform, a helmet and goggles. As for an alibi—well, you are supposed to be here all the time with me, aren't you? If you're ever questioned, I shall give you an alibi, my sweet.'

I kept silence. I was trying to work out where Rose had left her car, and how soon Sid could get back. If I could induce Toby to unbuckle my wrists, I might be able to free Hob, and together we could overcome Toby and get away before Sid returned . . .

Toby sighed and got up to wind the clock and re-set the hands. I breathed more freely for his absence. He stacked plates and took them out to the kitchen. I tried to shift the belt round my wrists, and failed.

'Got any sweets, Sarah?' That was Toby, rummaging in the kitchen. I didn't reply. He came back in, biting a biscuit, and holding a carton of glacé cherries.

'Why don't you go and feed the hens?' I asked. If only Toby would go out into the yard, I could get across to Hob even though his wrists were tied separately to the arms of his chair, he might be able to release me, and then we could arm ourselves against Toby's return . . .

'Damn the hens!' Toby was restless. He started on the cherries, glanced at his watch,

57

at the clock, and tapped the barometer. He switched on the radio, but it was as dead as usual. There were only children's programmes on the television, so that didn't please him, either.

In leisurely fashion he stripped off his shirt and trousers in order to pull on a pair of dark blue overalls. His brogues went neatly at the foot of the stairs, to be replaced by heavy boots. He tried on the helmets and set one aside for himself, combing his hair to lie straight back. He looked less civilised wearing overalls.

He ran his hands through my hair, and I shivered. Bending low over me, he held my head steady so that he could kiss my lips.

'You're a plucky little thing, aren't you?' he murmured. 'I quite fancy you, you know that? I wasn't pretending when I made up to you; in fact, I nearly came into your bedroom last night . . . just to see what you look like, stripped.' His hands fumbled at my waist, pulling my sweater up over my breasts. I kept my eyes ahead.

'You've got everything in the right place,' he said, 'And in the right proportion. I like a bit of spirit in my girls. Now why don't you . . .?'

'No,' I said, and stared through him.

He got hold of my sweater with both hands and although I tried to keep my arms to my sides, he pulled it up and right over my head, leaving it dangling down my bound arms over my back. He released the catch on my bra, and pulled it forward to hang at my waist. I continued to stare ahead, though I felt my cheeks flame. I would not show fear, or let him see that anything he chose to do would hurt me. If my breasts were not as large as Rose's, they were well-formed and worth looking at, so let him look!

He chuckled, and ran his finger over my nipples until they grew taut. I tried to give no sign that I had felt him touch me. I could feel his breath smooth my cheek as he leaned over me; I leaned back against my chair, pressing myself against the wood. He picked a glacé cherry out of the carton, split it open and fitted it over one of my nipples. Then the other. I felt blood seep from my head, and then return in a hot flush. I gulped. My cheeks quivered in an effort to repress tears.

Toby bent over me. He put one hand round my breast and started to lick at a cherry. I stared over him, and my eyes met Hob's. Ashamed, I withdrew my eyes from his, and then forced myself to stare back. The muscles round his eyes contracted in a smile as he saluted my self-control. He looked as if he understood how I felt about that . . . that thing . . . that criminal . . . licking at my breast. Fighting to keep my mind away from Toby, I concentrated on Hob.

If his hair were trimmed, and he were put into some decent clothes, I wouldn't be sorry to be seen out with him. Even with his eyes crinkled up, you could see he wasn't all that old; maybe thirty-five or so. He had an intelligent, good-humoured face. A well-used face. Not one kept in a window for display, but one that reflected what its owner felt about things.

I smiled back. It wasn't much of an effort; more of a grimace, in fact, but it was worth it. Hob grinned at me, and suddenly Toby's action seemed not evil, but mischievous. I found I'd been holding my breath and let it out. Toby teased off the second cherry and ate it. I tried not to look. It was far better to keep my eyes on Hob.

Toby started to nibble at my sticky, sweet breast. Momentarily I closed my eyes and shuddered. Then forced myself to look at Hob again. He was serious now, watching me. Caring what happened to me. Toby had tied his wrists to the chair, but had first pulled down the sleeves of his sweater so that his skin would not be marked. I began to think about the white band on Hob's wrist, where he had once worn a watch. Where he must have worn a watch until recently, for it would only take a few days in the sun to tan that tell-tale band of white skin.

Therefore, Hob must have worn a watch until a few days ago. Only, tramps didn't wear watches; they sold them for food.

Another thing. His beard had been trimmed

recently, even if his hair had been allowed to grow too long for my taste. I knew something about beards because my boss had grown one that year and had been forever snipping at it with a pair of nail scissors so as to keep it neat. Hob's beard was neat; no scissors had been found on him when he arrived at Elm Tree House, but he must have possessed a pair, or money enough to go to a barber, until quite recently.

My conclusion was that Hob hadn't been on the road for long—perhaps only for a few days?

I told myself that I was trying to upgrade Hob to the status of ordinary citizen because it was more comforting to think of my companion in misfortune as someone temporarily down on his luck, rather than as a tramp. As for his being mentally deficient, I had long ago made up my mind that it was an act. I decided that I would very much like to have half an hour alone with Hob, so that I could question him about himself. I thought it might be a most interesting session.

A sharp tug on my nipple caused me to double up. Toby had bitten me. I hung my head until I was sure I could school my face to show indifference. Toby stood up, and went to look out of the window. He had left me naked to the waist, and there was nothing I could do about it. The late afternoon sun gilded the edge of Granny's favourite picture, a water-colour of a local beauty spot. I looked at that, rather than face Hob. It was a river scene, cool and serene. The sunlight caught the edge of a bevelled mirror, and acting as a prism, set a rainbow shimmering on the wall.

Toby's bulk filled the doorway, ominously. I risked a quick glance at Hob, who was looking at the clock. I was glad that he wasn't looking at me any longer. I wanted to creep into a corner and wash myself clean. My feet hurt.

Toby tested the windows, dragging them shut if they were open, and slamming the catches into place. In spite of the open front door the room felt like a prison to me. He trod heavily out into the kitchen, to test the back door. He ought to know that it was locked, for he'd removed the key himself. I'd got as far as trying to inch myself out of my chair when he returned, and pressed me back. He had a pint of of milk with him.

'Drink this,' he said, and poured milk into a glass for me.

'I can't pick it up,' I said, hating to hear my voice come out unevenly.

'Say "please", Toby!'

'Please!'

He released my wrists. I massaged them, pulled up and clumsily fastened my bra, and settled my jumper into place before drinking the milk.

'Shall I give some to Hob, as well?' Toby asked.

I nodded.

'Say "please", Toby . . .'

'Please,' I repeated, like a child.

He poured out the milk and set the glass to Hob's lips. Hob drank, his eyes on mine. I think he was trying to tell me something— warn me? I couldn't think what to do, and time was running out on us. One thing was for sure, my feet were too painful for me to try running away again.

'Dress!' said Toby, throwing a blue uniform my way. I didn't move. He smiled, showing all his teeth. He fetched the big bottle of methylated spirits from the kitchen, and set it down near Hob on the polished table top. He uncorked the bottle, and poured a little of the liquid into the now empty glass of milk. We watched him, fascinated. From the mantelpiece he took down a candlestick which Grandpa had kept for emergencies, and checked the height of the candle stub which had been left in it. About an inch and a half. Carefully he dug a hole through the candle near the base, using a skewer, and threaded one end of a soft, cord-like string through it.

'Sid's good at cracking safes,' said Toby, 'And although we won't need to use any fuse to crack the safe at the Festival site, he came prepared.'

Toby set the candlestick on the table beside the bottle of meths and the glass, and then threaded the free end of the length of fuse through the string that bound Hob to the chair and finished up by winding it round his chest.

'Paraffin,' Toby explained, fetching a can from the kitchen. He took off the cap and let me sniff the contents. It was paraffin all right.

'No!' I cried. I guessed what he intended to do. I heard Hob's breath hiss as paraffin sloshed over him. His sweater became stained with dark patches of the liquid, and Toby completed the job by trickling it on his jeans and over his arms. Hob jerked against his bonds, but he had been well tied.

Toby explained what he was doing quite calmly, as if demonstrating an experiment to a class of children in school. 'We'll use meths for the fuse, though I shouldn't think it really necessary.' He tipped the bottle carefully over the length of fuse.

I pulled myself to my feet. I was trembling, and my feet hurt, but that wasn't important, now.

I pulled on the dark blue overalls, and had to belt them round me in great folds to make them fit. Granny's mending basket lay nearby, so I took a couple of pairs of thick bedsocks from it to pad out the boots, and make it easier for me to walk on tender feet. Toby grinned approval.

Hob said nothing, of course. He didn't look at me, and his hands were twisted round the arms of his chair. I wondered if he'd be able to get to work on his bonds with his teeth after we'd gone, and then dismissed the idea; Toby had forestalled any such manoeuvre by binding his shoulders to the back of the chair.

I tried walking; it wasn't comfortable, but it wasn't impossible. The gloves would disguise my hands, but at first I didn't see how I could balance the helmet on my head, for it was far too large. I fetched one of Granny's scarves and swathed it round my neck and over my head, pulling one fold up to cover my mouth.

'Not like that, poppet!' said Toby. He had a large piece of sticking plaster in his hand. He held my chin to kiss me taking his time over it, and then stuck the plaster over my mouth, firming it into place around and over my chin. Then he drew up the fold of scarf and buckled the helmet on. It was terribly heavy. My head trembled on my shoulders. Then came the goggles. I tried to breathe evenly. I felt smothered.

Toby handed me the gauntlets and I pulled them on. He buckled them at the wrists, but they were so large I thought I might be able to get them off, if I tried hard.

Then he pulled on his own helmet, goggles and gloves. His lips smiled at me, but the rest of his face was a blank.

We both heard the Mini crunch down the lane and round into the orchard. Sid was ready for us, already dressed in his uniform. I started for the door on stiff feet.

'Haven't you forgotten something?' asked

Toby. He pulled out a box of matches and struck a light. He laughed as he lit the candle. My nerves tightened as he took his time sticking more plaster over Hob's mouth—I suppose so that he could not try to blow out the candle or call for help if someone did chance to stray down the lane. Still moving in a leisurely fashion, Toby drew the curtains close, and bowed me out of the door before him. Hob raised his head to look at me. No trace of imbecility in his expression now. He was plainly afraid, and struggling to keep calm. His eyes widened to their limits, and his nostrils pulsated. His eyes deserted mine and went to the flickering candle. The room was dim, and shadows crowded the walls as Toby locked the front door.

'Sid—take her into the garage and stand her in a corner with your hands over her eyes till I give the word.'

Sid didn't argue, but did as he was told. I could smell his sweat and his bad breath as he crowded me into the garage and held me there. I started to count, knowing that my ordeal had barely begun, and fearing I would not be able to take it. Sid's gloves were enormous, blocking off light and air.

Then he released me, and prodded me into the driving seat of the van. I backed it out of the garage with him sitting beside me. Then he was locked into the body of the van by Toby, who came to sit with me.

'In case you are wondering,' said Toby. 'I hid the front-door key while you were in the garage. By way of insurance, as you might say. Only I know where I put that key, and I'm not going to tell anyone, even if we're caught. So don't get any ideas into your head about trying to attract the attention of the police while we're at the Festival, my sweet, or Hob will burn. Because even if you do get away from us, and find someone to talk to, and get them to believe you, and get them to come down here, they won't be able to get into the house to save your friend in time. That front door is solid oak, isn't it? Built to last . . . Even with axes and crowbars and the like, the police couldn't get through it in time to help your friend. No, your only chance of saving his life is to get me back here safely, so that I can unlock the door for you and pinch out the candle before it burns down.'

He sighed. A long, voluptuous sound. He stretched, enjoying himself. I saw he was one of those who enjoy taking risks, and being in danger.

'If anyone should chance to go down the lane,' he continued, 'they'll see nothing wrong in a house locked up and deserted. The cars are round in the orchard, at the back of the house—no one would see them if they came down the lane casually. The curtains are drawn, so no-one can see in. I estimate that if all goes well, we should be back within an

67

hour, and it will take about two hours for that candle flame to reach the fuse, so you see, Hob is perfectly safe if you drive properly. Of course if there is a hold-up, or anything goes wrong, then Hob will die. They'll find a charred corpse with a bottle of meths open in front of him. A tramp, who wandered in to shelter from the weather? Or perhaps they'll think it was you? You're much of a size, you two.'

It was a nightmare. Toby talked most of the way. Sometimes what he said got through to me, and sometimes it didn't. The van was heavy to drive, and needed all my concentration. My feet were tender and the heavy boots made me unresponsive.

Sid had done a good job on transforming the van. It had arrived in my yard painted a plain blue, with clear glass in the windows; he had covered the windows with some darkish plastic sheeting which allowed me to see out, but prevented people from seeing in. Over the windows he had stuck wire mesh, imitating proper armoured cars. I felt as if I were driving a fortress.

I was sweating from heat and fear, so I leaned over in an attempt to open the window beside me.

'None of that!' Toby cracked out, and I had to restore the window to its usual position.

I mimed sweat dripping from my forehead.

'Raise your goggles, if you like. No one can

68

see you.'

I raised my goggles, but still felt parboiled. The late afternoon sun had beaten all life out of the countryside. The inside of the van was close. I wondered what would happen if I were to faint.

'. . . amazing, really!' Toby was saying. I tried to concentrate. 'I thought you went for big men.'

What was he talking about? I turned a corner with care, and saw the tip of the big barn in Mr. Thomas' field shouldering up behind some trees in front of me.

'Take Sid, now!' continued Toby. 'He's a fine figure of a man, and plenty of women have fallen for him. I could understand you turning me down for Sid, but what you see in that little runt, I can't imagine!'

He was talking about Hob. How very odd! I wasn't physically attracted to Hob at all. How could I be? He was a tramp.

'I suppose it's that mop of curls that gets you. Fetching, at the moment, but he's likely to go bald early. Had you thought of that?'

I hadn't. I did think about it, and decided that even if Hob went bald, he'd still look kind and good-tempered, which was more than you could say for Toby if he were to lose his hair. Another thing, Hob was no teenager, and a man usually showed signs of losing his hair— if he was going to do so—about thirty. Hob didn't show any signs of losing his hair, so he probably wouldn't go bald.

'Do you really think a shrimp like that could make satisfactory love to you?' asked Toby.

I hadn't thought about that, either, and I would have said so, if my mouth had been free. I'd been sorry for Hob, he'd been kind to me, and had helped me when he could. There hadn't been anything more to it than that. I couldn't stand by and let a man be burned to death, even if I disliked him.

One thing I was sure of, though. Hob would never have humiliated me as Toby had done. And before he'd gone on the roads, he might have been attractive, even to one who normally only liked big men.

Was Toby jealous of Hob? I glanced at him, amused. Toby had been trying to run Hob down, and all he'd done was clarify my attitude towards the little man. It was quite clear to me now that I liked Hob as a person, and that I wouldn't even be averse to a flirtation with him some time—if we both got out of this affair alive.

'Stop!' said Toby suddenly. 'Draw in over there, under the trees.'

We hadn't reached the site yet, but I did as I was told. The sides of the road were littered with old vans, bangers that hadn't made it into one of the official car parks. A couple of tents could be seen through the leaves of the trees nearby, and there were plenty of beer cans and broken bottles strewn around. I sympathised

70

with Mr. Brent.

'No police here,' said Toby, looking around carefully. 'Rose said there wouldn't be, but it's best to be sure. The police are worried about Law and Order on the site, but can't spare enough men to do the job properly. Rose knows exactly how many men they've got, and how they're deployed. A good girl, our Rose. You needn't worry about them, though, because they certainly won't be worried about us. They'll greet us with open arms, you'll see!'

He opened his door and swung out of the cab onto the ground. He stood there, listening. Screaming jazz assaulted our ears. He walked a few paces this way and that, looking out for . . . what? I wondered if I could get out of the van on my side and make it into the woods before he returned. I lifted my boots from the floor and decided against it. I could never run fast in those boots, even if my feet were up to it.

A pale blue sports car slid into view at the end of the road, halted for a moment, and then crossed our vision. There was a small crossroads at that point. Rose's taffy head had been clearly visible in the driver's seat.

'That's it,' said Toby, checking his watch. 'Fifteen minutes from now.'

He got back into the cab and pulled a package from his pocket. It contained a badge, which he pinned to his uniform, and a false moustache kit. The moustache was big and

71

drooping, black in colour. I watched as he stroked it onto his upper lip, eyeing himself in the driving mirror as he did so. It altered what little could be seen of his face so that anyone asked to describe him after the robbery, would remember that he had a big black moustache, and that would be all. As Toby was fair himself, I thought it a good disguise.

'Good, isn't it?' he asked me, returning the driving minor to normal. He polished his badge with his sleeve. 'We've got their insignia on both sides of the van, too. Just stuck on, you know? Easy to remove when we've finished.'

I was doing sums in my head, and not liking the result. 'Fifteen minutes from now', Toby had said, and we'd been gone from Elm Tree House a good fifteen minutes already. Suppose the robbery were to take fifteen or twenty minutes—and although I didn't know the details, I assumed it must take that long to lift the money and put it in the van—then we had to return the way we came, and the whole operation would have taken us well over an hour. I was worried. I had believed Toby when he told me we'd be back in plenty of time to release Hob, but now I couldn't help wondering exactly how fast a candle burned, and how Toby had known that the stub he had lit would last two hours or more. It hadn't looked like two hours' worth to me—it had looked more like one and a half. Surely a candle burned at the rate of an inch an hour, didn't it?

'I'm sure my plan is fool-proof,' said Toby, half to himself. 'The police are concentrating on drug-users, fights, and keeping order. Most of them are in plain clothes, mixing with the crowd. Hardly any are on traffic control . . . just one or two, and they'll be pleased to see us rather than suspicious. Rose has just signalled that Mr. Thomas has taken his cut and removed himself and his guard of heavies, and the real Security men aren't due for another hour. We have Rose to thank for our hour's grace, by the way. The Security men were due to arrive as Mr. Thomas and his men left, but she phoned them and asked them to arrive one hour later. By the time they get here, we'll be back at Elm Tree House. No, it's foolproof!'

I was beginning to fear that Toby was quite callous enough to allow Hob to die, however much I cooperated. It seemed to me quite possible that he'd merely guessed how long it would take for the candle to burn down. The candle had been found on the mantelpiece, he'd not brought it with him. He'd found it, used it, and told me it wouldn't burn down to the fuse within two hours—just to make me cooperate. I began to sweat in earnest.

Toby checked his watch, and then produced two pairs of handcuffs from under the seat. I suppose he'd hired them with the costumes. The sun made them glint as he swung them free of each other.

'Merely a precaution,' he said. He clicked one pair of handcuffs round my left wrist and one round my right. They locked with difficulty over the bulky leather gloves, but didn't restrict movement. They looked like elaborate charm bracelets, tinkling as I put my hands back on the steering wheel. The still open halves of the cuffs swung free.

'Just to make sure you don't try to escape while we're loading up,' he said, pulling my goggles down over my eyes once more. 'You'll be locked in, of course, but we don't want you writing notes to passers-by, or running off in search of the police. Mind you, I'm probably being over-anxious, locking you in like this, but as I've got the cuffs, I might as well be safe as sorry. I don't know why it is that I don't trust you, but I don't. You won't forget that you hold Hob's life in your hands, will you? And that I hid the key to the door of the house, and that I will never, never tell anyone where I put it, even if you do escape?'

I remembered. I shook my head. Various schemes had been running through my mind about making a dash for it when we got to the site, but I abandoned them. Not even Sid knew where Toby had hidden the key, and I knew Toby meant it when he said he wouldn't reveal its whereabouts if he got caught.

Toby pulled the cab door to. A fly buzzed against the windscreen, and my goggles misted over. I adjusted them, and the cuffs clinked together.

Toby had found himself a truncheon. He started to tap it against one gloved gauntlet. I couldn't keep my eyes off it. He was smiling.

I felt sick. I thought, Oh God, he's quite capable of killing someone with that thing!

'Now!' said Toby.

I slid the van down the lane, and turned left. A hundred yards further on a uniformed policeman waved me into a bumpy field, crowded with parked cars. There was a police car parked near the entrance. Empty. A few caravans stood at the far end, in front of a shanty town of tents. The left hand side of the field was edged with a fence of corrugated metal sheeting, pierced at intervals by some shaky-looking sentry-type boxes; presumably these acted as gates to the Festival proper, which was being held in the next field. Sound waves beat on the van now that we were closer, as a jazz band did its best to deafen everyone within five hundred yards. I felt I ought to congratulate whoever had been responsible for the amplification. He was a genius. The place was adrift with litter. The field had been churned up and the mud had set hard in the sun. Motor-bikes snarled in a maze of hot metal at the far end of the field, and there was a stink of frying oil in the air.

'The first big caravan at the end of the line of gates,' said Toby. He spoke between smiling lips.

People were coming and going across the field. A bunch of officials had coagulated roughly half-way between the gates and the caravan which Toby had pointed out to me, and which I now saw bore a banner marked 'Office'. A pale blue sports car was parked under some trees nearby, together with half a dozen other cars in a roped-off enclosure which was probably reserved for officials. The field on our right was also full of cars and tents and here and there were stands for litter bags, all overflowing.

A bearded man appeared at our side and shouted something. Obviously one of the officials, and equally obviously, unsuspicious. He looked pleased with himself and the way the Festival was going. He was probably very relieved to see us, especially since Mr. Thomas had withdrawn his men.

'Turn it round,' directed Toby. 'Reverse so that our back doors are right up to their office.'

I complied.

'Not so close!' cried the bearded man, jumping about and waving his arms. 'Leave us room to get in and out!' A middle-aged, sharp-eyed man who looked like a PR type, came out of the caravan, and left the door open. At Toby's signal I moved the van some two paces forward. It was hard work pulling it round in that heat. My feet hurt. I took them off the pedals and killed the engine.

'Leave it running!' hissed Toby, and waited until I had re-started it. Then he clicked the free ends of the handcuffs to the rim of the steering-wheel. I could slide my hands round the wheel, but not remove them from it. I ground my teeth in frustration. Toby leant over me to test that the window was wound up to the top. It was. Then he eased himself out of the van, and locked both doors—his and mine.

I told myself that I was glad he'd closed his door after him, as it was hardly possible to hear yourself think with it open. I pulled on the sleeve of my overall until I could catch a glimpse of my watch. We'd been gone thirty-five minutes. My stomach began to play me up, and I wondered what would happen if I were sick.

The van shifted as Sid got out of the back. I watched in the driving mirror as he and Toby went together into the Office. There was a huddle of men around the office door, laughing and joking. They were all relieved to see the back of the money.

The great field in front of me was still reasonably quiet. The knot of officials by the gates split up, half coming our way and half going through the gates into the Festival site itself. They were mostly youngish men. Hefty, strong men. I was surrounded by people who could help me, and I couldn't communicate with them.

If I were to tear the plaster from my mouth,

get the window open and yell to them that there was a robbery in progress, how would they react? As Toby said, they would only laugh.

I looked at my watch. And panicked. Perhaps that was why Toby had put the cuffs on me; perhaps he had guessed that I would panic. The van was big, and the seat broad, but I tried again and again to turn the handle that opened the window I tried with my elbow and with my foot. And couldn't. I found I was crying with frustration. Of course I could tear the plaster from my mouth and yell, but who would hear me, with doors and windows shut fast, against that cacophony?

Forty minutes had gone by since we had left Elm Tree House. The doors of the van behind me opened and shut again. Both Toby and Sid had brought out a package and placed it in the van. The trouble was that they had to take the silver and the coppers as well, and coins were not only heavy but bulky. It might take several trips to shift the lot.

A young woman in a frilly skirt which swished around her ankles walked past, carrying a big brown teapot. She smiled up at me. I knew she couldn't see me properly; she was just being friendly. I watched her out of sight. What wouldn't I have given to be her at that moment?

Forty-five minutes. I began to fidget, and to try to clear my throat. The door of the van behind me opened, and two big packages were dumped in. What were they? Briefcases? Boxes? And the doors clanged shut on them once more. My nerves were jumping. I wished I'd learned how to smoke, and then I remembered I hadn't any cigarettes, and in any case I couldn't use my mouth . . .

The girl in the swinging skirt came back again, shaking drops from the now empty teapot. She must have tipped the tea-leaves on the ground at the back of the caravan. She went back into the Office. The group of officials were almost on us now. Toby and Sid would be heavily outnumbered if anyone did give the alarm.

Fifty minutes. Fifty minutes, plus fifteen to get back; it ought to be all right, if only we could get away now.

Why didn't they come? There had only been an interval of five minutes between trips before.

Fifty-two minutes. The jazz band fell silent, and was accorded round after round of applause. Several people drifted through the gates into our field. There was a big refreshment tent at the far end. A man in a cook's apron came out of the back of the tent and stood there, looking around. A big, paunchy man, rather like Sid.

Fifty-three minutes. What was keeping them?

There was an eerie silence. What was

79

happening? An interval? If so, then perhaps the field would soon be flooded with people, all watching as we drove through them. There were enough people to see us go, as it was . . . I started to count them. Five, seven, ten, fourteen . . .

Fifty-four minutes. A thump on the back of the van, and voices. Sid and Toby, making small talk. The weather had treated the Festival right, hadn't it? See them next year? Not at this site? No? Well, they'd be in touch, no doubt. Farewells.

Sid climbed into the back of the van and Toby locked him in, in leisurely fashion.

Fifty-five minutes. My fingers were clenched around the wheel.

'. . . back on the job!' laughed Toby. He climbed in beside me, and slammed his door shut. I rattled my handcuffs, and he released me from the wheel.

I didn't need him to tell me what to do. I threw the van into motion as if I'd done it every day of my life. Bump, bump. Not too fast, or I'd do the van an injury. Fifty-five minutes plus fifteen . . . it ought to be all right. We ought to get back in time.

An exclamation from Toby. An oath.

What?

People were milling through the turnstiles and I was having to drive slowly to avoid them. They saw nothing wrong in our presence in the field, so why should they get out of our way?

'Put your foot down!' shrieked Toby, and I was so shattered to hear hysteria in his voice that I did as I was bid. My palm found the horn, and people scattered as the van leaped forward, lurching over the rutted surface.

'Oh, my God!' Toby was saying, over and over. I couldn't understand what he was on about. I'd never heard him call on God before, and it sounded all wrong, coming from him. The remnants of a Christian education in me objected.

Then I saw it, too. An identical dark blue van, painted with exactly the same insignia that Toby had pinned on his uniform, was lurching into the field towards us!

My throat contracted. My foot slipped off the accelerator, and the van slowed.

Toby yelled at me, and I remembered Hob. It was an hour since we had left him It must be. Fifteen minutes to get back, and . . .

I stamped on the accelerator, and the van shot forward, throwing Toby against the cab door. I clung to the wheel and half stood on the accelerator. I had to get the van out of the field before the other one—the genuine security van—should tumble to the deception.

What had gone wrong? Why had they come early? Or were we running late?

A crowd of youngsters ran in front of the van. I swerved to avoid killing them. One screamed. A young girl, no more than twelve. I think it was Taney Touch from over Bentley way. It looked as if she'd hurt her ankle as she fell, but I had no time to worry about her.

'Step on it!' screamed Toby.

I wanted to scream back that I was doing everything that I could. We passed the other blue van. I could see faces staring at us, dimly; helmeted, Martian faces. I suppose we looked the same to them.

Out of the field. Bump. Bump. The policeman was looking puzzled, hand to mouth, but he wasn't running for his car, as he ought to have been.

'God! They've turned—they're following us!'

I risked a glance in the mirror. The van was turning, and the policeman—yes, at long last he had tumbled to it that something was wrong. He was doing the wrong thing, though. He was running towards the genuine Security van, with his hand up to stop them, instead of running for his car.

We were in the side road. I could turn left or right, or go straight on at the cross-roads. Right led to home, but that road was straight and you could see down it for miles No chance of eluding pursuit on that road.

'Lose them!' yelled Toby. 'You'll go to prison, too, if we're caught!'

I tried. As I turned left I saw the van lumber after us, the policeman running at its side. He looked worried, and so he should. In a moment he'd run for his car and presumably radio for help, and that would mean road blocks, reinforcements . . . We were running along a densely bordered, winding lane, which dipped and heaved itself over ridges. I knew it well. But the van clung to us. Now and then I caught a glimpse of the road behind the van and thought I saw another car following but it wasn't the police car, so I guessed it was that of a passing motorist.

A badly metalled lane. A straight strip of well-made road on which I sent the speedometer needle flickering to seventy. Right, and right again, sharply. We used to picnic in that field on the left, because it was sheltered and a stream ran across it.

A wood. A long slim road with a family car parked on the verge; mother and father looking for early blackberries, the children playing Last Across. One of them very nearly lost the game—permanently.

'They're still behind us!' breathed Toby.

Another wood. There were tracks through this wood which I had driven over as a child in Grandpa's ancient Morris. The last couple of days of good weather favoured us, making the tracks hard enough to bear the van. I took a sudden sharp turn into the wood, crashing over some brambles on to one of the broader tracks between the trees. It was just as I had remembered it, except that I had usually seen it from a lower level in the Morris. A junction of tracks. Straight across, because I knew now what to do.

'Why didn't you turn, you fool!' screamed Toby.

I shook my head, wordlessly. There was no way I could explain.

Hob! My God, I'd forgotten him! Are you all right, Hob? What is the time? We're miles from home . . .

'Bloody . . . bloody . . .!' He went on shouting it. So the other van was still behind. I had maybe a hundred yards lead, which was a lot in a wood. I was fast approaching a place where I could get back onto another road. I slowed down. Over the brambles into the road. Stop. Reverse. Back into the wood along the way we'd come, and slash . . . straight into a thicket of holly, driving right into it . . . through it. The paintwork on the van would be scratched to hell, but that didn't matter.

Stop the engine. Silence buzzed in my ears. Listen.

We froze in our seats, Toby with his arm uplifted, the truncheon dangling from his wrist, and I trying to get some air through my nose and into my lungs to still my heart.

Time to sit still.

CHAPTER THREE

We waited. A fly had somehow found its way into the tightly closed cab of the van. It flittered its way across the windscreen, rasping at my nerves.

Cautiously Toby leaned on the handle of the window beside him. He slid it down carefully, his other hand firm against the glass.

The blue nose of the genuine security van blustered its way across our line of vision, paused to consider the tracks our wheels had made when crushing through brambles to get onto the road, and decided to follow the false trail which I had set for them. We strained our eyes to see through the screen of holly bushes, watching the broad end of the van lumber onto the road and move off to the left.

Suddenly, I was trembling, and my face was cold with sweat.

Toby said, 'I'll see if Sid's all right. He was making a lot of noise back there. Maybe our cargo's broken loose!' His tiny joke relieved the tension. He clambered down, leaving his door open. I pushed up my goggles and tried to wipe sweat off my face with gauntleted hands. I could feel the van shift as Toby unlocked the back doors and then I heard Sid's voice raised in complaint.

Air! I needed air! I tested my door, but it

was still locked. I pushed myself over Toby's seat and let myself down onto the turf of the wood. My knees threatened to go limp. The faintest of breezes rustled leaves in the trees overhead, and birds sang. Without thinking of any possible consequences, I eased off my gauntlets so that I could rid myself of helmet and scarf. I tore the strapping from my mouth to gulp breaths of fresh air. My hair clung wet to my head. I ran my fingers through it and dried my face and neck on the scarf.

I felt stunned. Presently I went back into the bushes. I heard Toby and Sid laughing as they did the same. Their laughter was loud and uncertain. I couldn't laugh. In my fear, and my excitement during the chase, I had overlooked the fact that I had committed a number of crimes. In the eyes of the Law, I was now as guilty as Toby and Sid. If only I had allowed the real security van to catch up with us, surely they could have sent someone to the cottage to rescue Hob!

Hob! What was the time?

Alarmed, I found we had been away from the house for one hour and sixteen minutes.

'Toby!' I called his name as I made my way back to the van. 'We must be getting . . .'

And there I stopped, for during the few minutes that I had been out of sight, another car had come up behind us. The security van must have been followed all the way here; I remember glimpsing this elderly sports car during the chase. It must have fallen behind during the time it took us to slash through the wood, and had only now caught up with us. We were trapped.

Toby and Sid were standing beside the van, still in their disguise. The back doors of the van were unlocked, and the packages of money in plain view. The sports car had picked a slightly different path through the wood from that taken by us and the genuine security van, and it was passing the holly thicket on our side, so that they could not fail to see us.

'Christ!' said Sid, lumbering into a run. He ran away from the van, diving into the cover of the holly thicket.

Toby said nothing, but checked that his goggles were well down over his eyes before following him.

I screamed, hands to ears. The sports car had stopped and was backing away from the road and safety . . . backing towards the van and Toby and Sid . . . backing into danger. In the driving seat sat the wild-bearded young man who had greeted us at the Festival site, and beside him sat the young girl in the frilly skirt. She looked both scared and excited.

'Oh, pray God, no!' I cried, knowing exactly what was going to happen a second or two before it occurred. The girl looked across and saw me. I saw her mouth open to say something to the man beside her. I wanted to scream a warning to them to drive forward—

on—away —to fly for their lives. Toby burst out of the bushes behind them. He raised his truncheon and swung it, bringing it down on the back of the bearded man's head and neck. I closed my eyes and turned away, gagging.

The girl screamed. She had a good pair of lungs on her. And through the scream I heard metal crunch as the car ran into a tree. The engine coughed and died. There was silence.

I hunched my shoulders to my ears and waited for further screams. There were none. No screams, no yells. Nothing but the sound of men's heavy breathing.

I took my hands from my ears and peered over my shoulder. Toby and Sid were bending over the driver and his girl, neither of whom were moving, Toby lifted his truncheon and brought it down again, hard—this time on the girl. There was a squelching sound. I stumbled behind a tree and threw up.

There were further noises behind me. Dragging noises. I took no interest in them.

Eventually Toby came and hauled me out. I tried not to look at the sports car, but I couldn't seem to help myself. The man lay slumped across the wheel, and flies were busy on the back of his neck. The girl had been pulled out of the car and lay on her face with legs and arms twisted; her pretty skirt awry above her knees. A wedding ring glinted on her left hand, and there was blood on her long fair hair. Sid was doing something to the sports car.

'Your helmet!' rapped Toby. 'Goggles—scarf—gauntlets?'

The front of his overalls and his gauntlets were spattered with blood. There were flecks of blood on his false moustache and cheeks, too.

'Blood!' I said stupidly.

He slapped me, and all I could think of was that now I would have blood on me, too. He thrust me into the cab of the van, and went to look for my things. In the wing mirror I could see Sid run away from the sports car, which seemed to erupt into flame. I felt him climb into the back of our van as I watched the sports car blaze. A funeral pyre for a jazz fan.

The girl's body wouldn't be touched by the flames, which was a pity. At that moment I wished I was lying in her place, close to the earth, where no more trouble or grief could reach me.

Toby was speaking to me. I turned my head stiffly, trying to make sense of what he said. He might as well have been speaking Greek for all I could tell. Impatiently he crammed my helmet back on my head and buckled it lightly. Goggles over that. Scarf round my throat and mouth. The helmet slid sideways, because it wasn't padded out with the scarf underneath it. I didn't bother to straighten it. I was all used up.

He dragged me from the driver's seat and

took the wheel himself. All I had to do was direct him. I sat there, dumbly indicating that he should turn right or left at each crossroads. His gauntlets left reddish stains on the driving wheel. A fragment of my brain was still working, and it informed me it would be wiser to obey him rather than become his third victim. We met three cars on the side roads, but none of them took any notice of us. The most dangerous stretch was the half mile or so of main road we must use to get to our lane, but even there we were lucky. We were lost in a stream of caravans and family cars returning from, or going away on holiday.

At last the lane down to the cottage. Bump, bump. Take it carefully. Would he kill me as soon as we got back home? I had witnessed a double murder, and I had been the driver of the getaway vehicle. I knew too much to live, and surely my usefulness was over, now that I had guided him back to the cottage?

And Hob? Yes, of course Hob would have to die, too, if he wasn't already dead. I found I didn't greatly care if he was. Perhaps it would be better for him if the candle had already burned down to the fuse and turned him into a human torch. It would be over all the sooner for him.

I waited patiently while Toby parked the van in the garage, and fished in the flowers by the front door for the key. I didn't even hurry myself to get inside once he had unlocked the front door.

Hob was still alive, but he looked ten years older than when I had last seen him, even in the dim light of the darkened cottage. As Toby drew the curtains, I saw that there were grey lines engraved on Hob's face, and smelt his sweat. He had strained against his bonds until he had exhausted himself. He had been through a piece of hell while we had been away, but I had no energy left to be sorry for him.

The candle flame was flickering around the fuse which would turn him into a human sacrifice, but I seemed unable to move fast. One, two, three, four paces to the table in my heavy boots. I bent over, steadying myself with one hand against the table while I carefully licked my fingers; and pinched out the candle flame. Where were my gauntlets? Had Toby rescued them for me? Did it matter?

Then, without meeting Hob's eyes, or attempting to take off my heavy clothes, I climbed the creaking wooden stairs to my bedroom, to the little slip of a room in which I had spent so many carefree nights as a child.

It was no surprise that Toby should follow me. His eyes flashed, his teeth grinned at me, at the mirror, at nothing. I took off the scarf, helmet and goggles. Then slipped out of the boots and unzipped the overalls. I was still wearing normal clothes, underneath. My face looked strange as I scrubbed my cheek clean, watching myself in the mirror. Was that me? It didn't look like me, so stary-eyed and peaky.

Toby let me lie on the bed, and then tied my wrists and ankles to the four corners. 'Comfortable?' he asked me. I stared through him.

He went out, leaving the door open. I remembered then that I hadn't asked him to set Hob free. I thought it wouldn't have done any good to ask. I slept.

*   *   *

I was drifting under the surface of sleep, uneasily aware of a disturbing dream, yet not anxious to wake. In the next second my eyelids had shot open, and sleep was gone for good. The room was murky in the dusk, but familiar. I was lying in an uncomfortable position. I tried to turn over, but the tug of cords at wrists and ankles prevented me from doing so.

Then I remembered. I remembered the bare, bloody neck of the cheerful young man from the Festival . . . the glint of the wedding ring on the hand of the girl who had delighted in frilly skirts . . . Hob's face grey with fear and exhaustion . . . and my own lack of future.

I became angry. Why should I have to die so young and so inexperienced? Why should this have happened to me?

I heard men's voices, and feigned sleep.

It was Toby speaking, in the next room.

'. . . the only question is where? The tickets can't be changed now, because it would look suspicious. And I'm not going into a Travel Agency around here to ask for them to be changed. They'd remember me and maybe start asking questions. No, we must stick to our original plan.'

'I don't fancy staying two more nights here, that's all.' It was Sid speaking. The communicating door between the bedrooms had been left open, and I could hear every word. Either they thought me asleep, or else they didn't care whether I heard them or not.

'Even Rose shouldn't object to this bed,' said Toby. I heard my grandparents' double bed protest as he bounced on the springs.

'We're too close, here!' argued Sid. 'The alarm will be out for us, and if we're seen . . .'

'The alarm isn't out for us, though, is it?' Toby's voice grew faint. Footsteps. He was in the bathroom, and then the footsteps returned. 'We are friends of Miss Sarah Long, whom she's invited to stay for a couple of nights; that's me and Rose. As for you, you can keep out of the way if anyone does happen to come down the lane, although it's not likely that anyone will. Rose and I will sleep in this bed, and you can kip down on the sofa by the fire.'

'I didn't know you was going to murder anyone,' Sid sounded injured. 'You might have warned me.'

'I didn't know either, did I?' Toby was

impatient. I heard the rasp of a window catch. 'These windows are far too small for anyone but a child to get through, but I think we'll secure them to their bed, just in case. I did think of shoving him in the back of the van for tonight, but on reflection I think I'll be happier having them both under my eye tonight. He's a slippery little devil, and there's all sorts of tools in that garage which he might be able to get at if he were free.'

'But if you lock him in the van? Why not?'

'We don't want him damaging himself, do we?' Toby laughed coarsely, and I felt prickles of sweat congeal on my back. He approached the door between the two rooms; I could hear him tinkering with the lock, trying some keys in it. I could have saved him time and trouble by telling him that the lock had been broken years ago, but he eventually found out for himself that it was no good.

'I reckon my cut ought to be bigger,' said Sid. 'Considering what's happened.'

'You'll get what we agreed on at the beginning, and like it.'

'I didn't agree to murder.'

'You helped. And the only way for you to get out of this safely is to continue to do as I say. Got it?'

'We could just leave them here when we go. All tied up, to give us a good start.'

Toby sighed. He abandoned the lock and went to check on the window. That, too, was small. I hadn't been able to get out of it since I was ten. 'They know us by sight, and they could split on us if we left them alive. You want to come back someday, don't you? So we use them as scapegoats. We dress them in the clothes we used for the job, and we leave the truncheon behind, with his fingerprints on it. We leave the van behind, locked in the garage. We don't clean the transfers off it, but we do clean it of our fingerprints. We leave behind some of the money we stole, and we make it look as if the rest got burned; yes, I like that idea. We stage it so they'll think the villains fell out after the robbery . . .'

'But there were three of us. They know that. And you've burned your overalls already, so . . .'

'So the driver got away? Who cares? They can look for him for ever, can't they? But they'll be looking for a small man, and as he doesn't exist and never did exist, they won't get very far.' They tramped back into the other room. Their voices were fainter now; I think Toby was trying his bunch of keys on the lock of the door which shut the big bedroom off from the top of the stairs. 'We arrange the scene very carefully,' he was saying. 'We get him to kill her first, using one of the knives in the kitchen. We wreck her car and set fire to it; make it look like his share of the money burned in the car. Then we sprinkle him with meths or whisky, and stage a suicide for him.

Hanging would be easiest, I think, though hanging's too good for him . . . all the trouble he's caused me. The cops will read it right, trust me for that! Thieves fall out, one stabs the other, sets alight to the money in the getaway car, and kills himself. Perfect!'

There was a silence while Sid thought it over. I heard Toby say "Tchah" as he discovered none of his keys would fit that lock, either, and then Sid started back at the beginning again.

'I still don't like the idea of staying here for another two nights. It's too close.'

'All right. Say we stay here tonight. We'll have to, anyway. It would be too risky to move now, and we've nowhere to go to. I've already given up my flat and Rose has moved out of her digs. I don't want to risk trying to get into hotels where we're not known, and I don't suppose you do, either. We're perfectly safe here. But tomorrow we'll set the scene, and drive off back to London, you in my car and me with Rose. We take our time on the journey and arrive at the airport terminal at Heathrow some time during the evening. We can meet up in the Departure Lounge . . . the Restaurant . . . anywhere. We spend the night at the Terminal; lots of people do, so we won't be noticed. Our plane leaves early the following morning, and heigho for sunny Greece, and a long holiday without money troubles. Is that better?'

'Ah, that's better. I don't fancy staying here two nights, that's all.'

They banged their way downstairs, just as another car drove into the yard. I heard a car door shut, and then Rose's voice raised in greeting. She sounded pleased with herself. I began to work on the cords that tied me to the bed. A quarter of an hour later I was a ball of sweat, my wrists and ankles were raw, and I was still tied to the bed. I started to cry, but no one heard me. No one cared whether I lived or died.

There was a lot of noise going on beneath me. Rose was calling to Toby to lay the table, and subsequently there was a great clatter of plates. I became aware that I hadn't eaten since breakfast, and that I was feeling faint from lack of food. And water. I would have given anything for a drink of water.

The electric light next door was switched on, and I opened my eyes to Rose standing in the doorway between the two rooms, looking down at me. She was carrying a suitcase.

I tried to ask her to help me, but my tongue wouldn't work. She hesitated, but didn't come into the room.

'How long have you been tied up?' she asked.

'Since we got back.' My voice sounded unlike me, hoarse and gritty.

She pulled a face, but did not release me.

'Water?' I requested, without much hope.

She glanced back over her shoulder. 'I don't think . . .' she began. And then, 'I'll ask him when I go downstairs.'

She disappeared from the doorway, and I heard her moving around next door, unpacking, going to the bathroom.

I said loudly, 'I shall wet the bed if you keep me tied up like this.'

'Heavens, no!' she cried, and I heard her rush to the stairs and clatter down them. There was the sound of an argument, and then Toby came back, with her. He was frowning. I could see his dilemma; he didn't give a damn if I wet the bed or not, but he didn't want to appear callous before Rose. He said, grudgingly, that I might go to the toilet, but I'd have to change back into my overalls first. He'd wait for me, and then tie me to the bed again for the night.

'Better not,' I croaked. 'If you don't give me something to eat and drink, and let me take some exercise so that I get my circulation back, then I'll not be able to stand by tomorrow morning.'

'So . . .?' he said, impatiently.

'Mr. Brent is sending some of his men down here tomorrow morning, to collect the hens. Remember? If I'm not around and about, and looking lively, they'll come enquiring for me, won't they?'

'You did this on purpose!'

Rose laughed. 'Don't be silly, Toby, dear! How was she to know? She's a sensible girl.

She drove you today, didn't she? She's going to get her cut, isn't she? So we can trust her to fool the farmer tomorrow morning. I really don't see why you thought it was necessary to tie her up like this in the first place.'

Toby untied the knots around my wrists and ankles without a word. He could have cut through the cord in a second, but no doubt he was preserving it intact for use at a later date. I tried to sit upright, and failed to make it.

'And Hob,' I bargained. 'I'll not play my part unless you release him, too.'

Toby gave me a measuring look, but nodded. Rose helped me off the bed. To do her credit, she liked this latest development as little as I did. She rubbed my arms and legs to get the circulation going again but was efficiency itself when it came to confiscating my clothes. Toby helped her empty my chest-of-drawers and remove my things into the double bedroom. Tears came into my eyes as I donned the hated overalls once more. I felt defeated.

'You poor thing,' she said, mistaking tears of rage for tears of pain. She offered me one of my own handkerchiefs, and helped me to the bathroom. When I came out, Toby had gone, and she was changing her scanty top for a long-sleeved blouse.

'Don't worry!' I grinned at her. 'I couldn't run away if I tried.'

'I know that, dear. I only wish Toby hadn't

99

thought it necessary to tie you up. I told him I thought he was being silly, but he's got the idea into his head that you're not to be trusted. You'll just have to bear with him until tomorrow.'

'Tomorrow?' I asked, not sure how much she knew of Toby's plans for Hob and myself.

'Only another twelve hours,' she nodded, retouching her makeup. 'We were supposed to be here right up to the time we left to catch our plane, but Toby thinks it best if we leave tomorrow instead.'

'You know he's going to kill us?' It sounded ridiculous, stated baldly like that, and I could see Rose didn't believe me.

'Oh no, dear! Toby wouldn't do a thing like that. We'll have to tie you both up when we go, naturally . . . but that's just to make sure we get a good start. We'll phone that farmer friend of yours from the airport, and ask him to call round on some excuse or other. He'll release you, but not before we're in the air. It won't matter what tale you tell then.'

So she didn't know about the murders in the wood. I thought about telling her, and then decided not to do so. If Toby had not told her, it was a fair guess he had not done so because he feared she might recoil from him if she knew. If I told her, she might or might not decide to help me, but the chances are that she would hardly be an effective ally against Toby and Sid. On the other hand, I might be able to

100

blackmail Toby into agreeing to let us go when he left, with the threat that I would otherwise have to tell Rose that he was a murderer.

She helped me down the stairs. Hob was still bound to his chair, facing the stump of candle and the length of fuse. The table had been laid for three.

'I said Hob had to be free, too!' Toby gave me a black look, but directed Sid to let the little man go.

Hob couldn't move when Sid had finished clearing away his bonds. I tried to help him stand, and failed. I started to cry again. Hob couldn't do much, but he managed to put one arm round my shoulders. By hauling on the table, I managed to pull him upright. He stumbled forward and collapsed, dragging me down with him. His face contorted with the agony of returning circulation.

Rose brought us a cracked cup with some of Granny's wheat wine in it. There was a lot of good in Rose. I took a couple of sips and gave the rest to Hob. Between us we massaged his arms and legs back to life. Toby didn't like Rose having anything to do with Hob, and he hauled her away to dish up supper. Hob was gasping with the pain. I got him to his feet, and with our arms round each other's shoulders, we stumbled up and down the room. He was about an inch taller than me, but his chest was deep and every inch of him felt hard. He stank of paraffin.

'Come and get it!' said Rose, plonking three plates of food on the table.

'What about us?' I demanded. 'We must eat, too.'

Toby sat down and started to eat, eyeing us. I thought he was spiteful enough to refuse my request, but in the end he jerked his head at Sid, and told him to get Hob into the overalls Sid had worn that day, and put Hob's paraffin-soaked clothes on the fire. Hob didn't like the idea; perhaps he guessed that we were to be set up as fall-guys. He shook his head violently, but it did no good. Sid laughed as he grasped Hob by one arm and peeled off his sweater. Hob shivered, and indicated he would prefer to retire to the kitchen to wash and dress himself in private.

'If you like,' said Toby indifferently. 'He can't get out of the back door; I've got the key.'

Sid threw the sweater Hob had been wearing onto the fire.

'Pouff!' said Rose, waving her hand in front of her nose. 'Take him out of here—he stinks!' She sat down and started to eat.

'What about food for us?' I asked.

Toby shrugged and said we might forage for ourselves if we liked. I followed Hob out into the kitchen, in time to see him prudishly close the toilet door on me. I grinned to myself. Hob seemed to be well-endowed, and it was a great pity we hadn't met under other circumstances.

It occurred to me that I might have enjoyed learning about sex from Hob. I threw a meal together and we ate at the kitchen table, sitting side by side. Hob looked comically shrunken in Sid's overalls, but his table manners were good, and he didn't slop his food about as Sid did. When I felt a little better, I told him why he had been put into Sid's overalls, about the double murder in the wood, and the plans Toby had to dispose of us. He nodded, his eyes robin-bright.

'No talking!' commanded Toby, from the doorway behind us. 'Finished eating? You look like twins, sitting side by side and dressed alike.' He laughed, unkindly.

'Tweedledum and Tweedledee, or Siamese twins, joined together in life and in death.' He dangled a pair of handcuffs. He made us stand, and clipped my right ankle to Hob's left. Then he pushed us into the living-room. I staggered and would have fallen if Hob had not caught at my arm. Toby told us to sit on the bench under one of the windows, where he could see us. And not to talk.

I didn't feel like talking when he could listen, anyway. I was trembling with rage and humiliation. I had never been any good at the Three-Legged Race at school. Hob put an arm round my waist and got me to the bench, somehow. When we sat, he left his arm round my waist, and I leaned against him, thankful that he no longer stank of paraffin.

The string that had bound Hob was now burning on the fire, as were my old jeans. The candle was back on the mantelpiece, and the meths bottle on the sideboard. On the table lay the remains of the meal the three conspirators had eaten, and several daily papers, which Rose must have brought with her. All there were busy scanning the newspapers; at first I thought they must be looking for reports of the robbery at the Festival, and then I realised that wasn't possible, for the daily papers would not contain news of that until tomorrow, the day on which Hob and I were due to die. But there must be something in the newspapers to arouse their interest, for Sid and Rose kept looking down at one particular spot on the page, and then looking over at us. Toby was staring at another paper, and pulling a face.

'I was right, you see!' said Rose to Toby.

He made an irritated gesture, sweeping the papers to the floor. He demanded what the hell she thought he ought to have done about it, then! She didn't answer, but picked up the newspapers, smoothed them out, folded them neatly and stacked them on the end of the table.

'Fool!' cried Toby. He snatched them from her, and, tearing them apart, he bunched each sheet separately and began to poke them onto the fire. Out of the corner of my eye I saw Rose tear a small piece from one sheet of newspaper and slip it into her pocket. Sid saw her, too, and was just working himself up to say something about it when she frowned at him, and asked if he wanted a cup of tea.

'I don't mind,' he said, diverted.

'Neither do I,' she said brightly, and began to chatter about who was going to do the washing-up and how she was looking forward to a good long holiday during which she wouldn't have to cook or clean or even think about preparing food.

Toby poked the last sheet of newspaper on the fire and coldly told her to shut up and get on with it. She made a face at his back, but obeyed.

When she was out in the kitchen, Sid turned the television on.

'What do you want that on for?' demanded Toby.

'The news!' said Sid.

'Idiot!' hissed Toby, and yanked the plug out of the wall, so that the television fizzled into silence.

'What do you want to do that for?' asked Sid.

'Do you want her . . .' he pointed to the kitchen, 'To hear about what went on in the wood?'

'But I'd like to know . . .'

'I've got a radio in my car. I'll slip out and listen to the news now, and you can slip out and listen to it later. I'll tell Rose just as much as I think she should know, and you'll tell her nothing more than I see fit to tell her. Right?'

Sid muttered that he supposed so.

I thought that maybe my idea about blackmailing Toby into letting us stay alive might work. I was also maliciously pleased that Toby had brought us into the living-room before I'd had time to wash up the plates Hob and I had used for supper. If we were prisoners, we might as well give the maximum amount of trouble.

Sid watched us sullenly while Toby went out to listen to the news. He didn't take his eyes off us once, except when Rose handed him a cup of tea. She didn't offer us any. Hob and I kept quiet as mice, except when one or other of us felt a limb beginning to stiffen and gave it a rub to keep the circulation going. Each time he had to remove his arm, Hob checked my face for permission to move, and each time he replaced it. I leaned against him and allowed myself to relax. The exertions of the day, the fear, the tension, and then the food all combined to make me sleepy. His curly head tickled the skin of my forehead. I jerked myself awake. Toby was sitting beside Rose, near the fire. Sid was nowhere to be seen; perhaps it was his turn to listen to the news? Both Toby and Rose were smoking, and the air in the room was becoming foul. I looked round to see if I could open the window behind us, and Hob beat me to it. The night air was chilly, but it revived me. I knew I ought to be worrying about important things like death, and how I could get some message to Mr. Brent, but the room was warm, and . . .

Rose yelped. Toby was teasing her, and although she was enjoying his teasing, she didn't like him playing with her in front of an audience.

'No . . . not now, you oaf!' she was saying.

'Come on . . . Come on!' he said, mumbling against her shoulder. He had her blouse undone, and his hands were . . .

I looked away, remembering what he'd done to me that afternoon. Out of the corner of my eye I saw Hob's hand, which had been lightly resting on his knee, ball into a fist. He would be remembering, too! I wondered what it was about Toby that made him need an audience when he pawed a woman. Hob's face had turned an unpleasant shade of purple. With rage. I risked a full glance at him. He was staring straight ahead, and holding himself rigid. His arm was equally firm around me. I wondered if he were the sort to have a coronary . . . and then the red began to retreat from his face, he took a deep, quivering breath, and forced himself to relax. I looked away from him, wondering at the depth of his reaction, because it looked to me as if he had been almost as strongly affected by Toby's sick caresses as I had been.

Thinking about Hob, I concentrated on the fire, and almost missed Sid's return, and low-voiced report. The flames were sinking, since no one had put anything on the fire for some time. The fire flickered and dissolved into a red haze.

Toby was pulling on my arm. 'Up, my beauty! Up!'

I shook my head, and blinked. The table was laid for breakfast, and Sid was laying blankets and sheets out on the settee . . . I recognised the bedclothes as the ones that had been on my bed. The clock said half-past ten.

Hob helped me to stand upright, with his arm still round my waist.

'Up the stairs!'

'We can't, like this,' I said. 'Take the handcuffs off. We can't climb the stairs two abreast, and we have to go to the bathroom.'

For a wonder, he agreed. He followed us up the stairs, waited till we'd finished in the bathroom, and then indicated that we both lie down on my single bed in the smaller bedroom. I was right in thinking that Sid had stripped my bed; he'd left us one skimpy blanket, and one thin pillow.

'There's some more blankets in one of the tea-chests,' I said. 'And pillows, as well.'

'Make do with what you've got. You can keep each other warm.'

The bed creaked as we lay down on it. Toby used both his pairs of handcuffs this time, one for each of us; with our left ankles secured to the rail at the bottom of the bed, we wouldn't be taking any midnight strolls.

'Sleep well, twins!' he said, in parting. 'You've fancied each other since you first met, so make your last night on earth a good one!'

He drew the curtains, switched off the light, and shut the door between the two bedrooms.

*　　　*　　　*

We lay there for a long time, just thinking and holding hands. How that had come about, I don't know. It had just happened. I could hear Toby and Rose arguing about something next door . . . something about it being wrong for him to tease her in front of other people . . . and then muffled squeaks and laughter as they had a session on the bed. It made me burn to think how my grandparents' bed was being misused. I tried to think what comments they might have made on the situation if they'd been alive, and failed to come up with anything that sounded even remotely possible. Then I burned at remembering how Toby had told us to spend the night. Luckily Hob wasn't the lecherous type.

He didn't move, but lay staring up at the ceiling, as I had done for many a long evening in my childhood and adolescence. I wondered if he saw the same faces in the cracked plaster that I used to see. For a while our room was dimly lit by the streaks of light which leaked round the door of the main bedroom. Then they disappeared, and the room became darker than before. I couldn't sleep, but I tried to keep still. For one thing, I didn't want to fall off the bed, and for another, I didn't want to put ideas into Hob's head.

Unfortunately, I was having difficulty dismissing those very same ideas from my head. My mind kept returning to the times when I had nearly lost my virginity with this and that boyfriend. I had hung on to it with some absurd idea of waiting for Mr. Right and marriage and all that. How stupid of me! I ought to have taken every one of those opportunities, and then I would at least have known what being a real woman was all about before I died.

A voice at the back of my mind insisted that it wasn't too late, and that I did have a chance to make up for lost time if I wanted to take it. The idea was worth consideration.

I had taken a fancy to Hob, as Toby had said. I did like him and I didn't dislike his appearance, although I thought his hair had been allowed to grow too long. In fact, I was quite fond of him, and I wouldn't have minded getting properly acquainted with him one day—if I'd had the chance.

The only thing was, that if you discounted that helpful retaining arm of his, Hob had never looked on me in the light of an easy lay. And indeed, why should he have done so? Tramps don't usually find that the ladies of the houses on which they call, are ready to offer their charms. But he wasn't an ordinary tramp, I told myself, and the circumstances were unusual.

'Hob!' I whispered. I felt rather than saw that I had his attention. 'I want to talk to you . . . Bother, I forgot!' I lapsed into silence, wondering how I could possibly explain my need to him. On his part he seemed to be attentive. He pressed my hand, which gave me an idea.

'Will you press my hand once for "Yes" and twice for "No": all right?'

One press. Yes.

'Are you a virgin?' What a stark way to blurt it out, I thought. How tactless could I get?

Two squeezes, and an interested turning of his body towards mine. He was quick on the uptake, wasn't he?

'Well then . . . shall we . . .?'

I pulled my hand away from him, and sat up. I began to unzip my overalls. He got the idea all right, and did the same to his. We groped for each other. He was furry-chested and his arms were strong. His mouth found mine, and he started to kiss me. I turned my face away, wanting sex, not love.

He froze. I could feel his heart beating against my ribs. He was excited. His body was ready, but he held back.

'Get it over with, you fool!' I hissed.

No. A definite withdrawal. He put his hand

111

on my breast, and pushed me gently away.

'I'm a virgin,' I said, forgetting the need for caution. 'I want to know what it's like before I die. That's all! Surely you can manage that for me!'

Cold air separated us. He zipped up his overalls and lay down again. I could hear him breathing quietly, in controlled fashion.

I wept angrily, but he took no notice of me.

I humped a shoulder at him, zipped up my overalls and monopolised our blanket. I was furious with him for refusing me and then, I grew furious with myself for having been so naive . . . and then mad at myself for having handled the incident so tactlessly. Hob had every right to feel insulted, and the odd thing was that his refusal had increased my respect for him, and not diminished it. If I'd only told him that I liked him instead of demanding satisfaction in that crude way . . .!

I reflected, between sobs, that I hadn't cried so much in my whole life as I had done in that one day. I told myself that I fully deserved everything that had happened to me. My vanity had led me to encourage Toby, and my selfishness had alienated Hob.

When I woke, it was early morning, grey and chilly. The room was filled with the dispiriting light of dawn. Hob was restless in his sleep, with one of his arms thrown over my body, and the other flung above my head.

A cockerel crowed in the yard beneath.

Trust him to wake me early on my last day on earth! Soon the hens, discovering that they had not been shut in last night, would bow and peck their finicking way out of the henhouse and into the yard, scratching and squawking, wanting their food.

I grabbed at the blanket just as it started to slide to the floor, and Hob started awake. His eyes blinked up at me, bemused with sleep, and then cleared to watchful intelligence.

'I'm sorry about last night,' I said, speaking softly. 'I was stupid and rude and all the rest of it. And selfish. I'm glad you've woken early, because I wanted to apologise.'

His eyelids relaxed. He picked up my hand, held the palm to his mouth and kissed it. I was to be reinstated in his good books.

'The stupid part of it is,' I went on in a rush, 'That, as Toby said, I do like you, very much. And if we'd had time to get to know each other, maybe it would have been even more than "like".' His eyes were very bright.

'Am I blushing?' I asked, trying to pretend I didn't mind if I was.

He treated me to one of his beautiful smiles, and settled the blanket back over my shoulders. I tried to relax, but couldn't. The light around the unlined curtains at the window was growing stronger every minute and every minute that passed took us closer to the time when Toby and Sid would make an end of me.

113

'How old are you, Hob?'

His hands flickered, twice, three, four times with one thumb tucked in. Thirty-six.

'Have you been a tramp for long?'

An amused negative.

'What did you do, before?'

He made a digging motion, and then inspected something small on the palm of his hand. I didn't understand. He tried again building a house with his hands, knocking it flat, and then digging. I still didn't get it. He checked my face for comprehension, shrugged, and wrote in the air, at full-length.

'You teach?' Doubtfully.

A qualified assent.

'What went wrong, then?'

He pointed to the other bedroom.

'Toby and Rose? You mean when Toby knocked you down? Well, I know that. What I don't understand is why you became a tramp.'

A violent negative. He wasn't a tramp.

I gave up. 'You are married?' I was hoping he'd indicate he wasn't.

A nod. A flicker of three fingers. A sweeping motion of both hands.

'You have been, but no longer?' A nod. 'It finished three years ago?' Another nod. He put both hands under his head and closed his eyes.

'Ah—she died?' Another nod. His eyes were sad, but clear of pain. He gestured to a bloodied scab on his hand, and to the white-washed wall.

I got that. 'Her blood was white . . . leukemia.' I knew I shouldn't ask the next question, but I had to know. 'Did she take long to die?'

'Yes.'

He turned his head away from me, intimating that he didn't want any more questions on that subject.

I have never been the jealous type. Correction, I had never known what jealousy was until Hob told me he'd been married. I was so miserable, and so angry that I wanted to hurt him, and knew that I'd only hurt myself if I did. At least my jealousy showed me what I really wanted.

I put my hand on his shoulder, at the base of his neck.

What now? his eyes asked me.

'I know what I want to say, but I'm not sure how to say it. The men I've come across till now are as selfish as I am; they're all out for what they can get and the Lord help any girl if she's unlucky enough to get herself pregnant. I can't remember any of them doing anything for anybody else, unless they saw a profit in it. I suppose my attitude was the same as theirs, so perhaps it's not surprising that I only came across that kind of man. I accepted their philosophy, because it was the philosophy of all my friends, and of the people I worked with. At least, I accepted it up to a point, because I never could bring myself actually to go to bed with any of them. I suppose I'd got into the way of thinking that any other kind of man was too dull to think about. I wonder what would have happened if I'd met you under normal circumstances?' He smiled a little, as if to say I'd probably not have noticed him.

'You frightened me so much at first,' I said. 'I had a bad scare from a tramp when I was a child, and tramps have been bogeymen to me ever since.' We exchanged smiles. 'It's quite true, what Toby said, about my liking big men. Usually, that is. I liked to look up to them. It made me feel secure, and looked after . . . like the way you make me feel. I'm glad we met. I want to say "thank-you" for helping me yesterday. And for last night. I put it very badly, then, but I'd like you to know how I feel about you.'

He laid one of his hands over mine, and rested his head against it. I thought, it's now or never. He'll not risk another rebuff. I wasn't too sure that I liked kissing a bearded man, but it was something I had to do. I kissed him once, and he didn't respond. Not at all. He just lay there watching me. His eyes closed as I kissed him the second time, though, and the third time I felt him stir beneath me. I still wasn't sure about the beard; it was springy, unexpected. He began to kiss me back. I giggled nervously, but my arms went round his

116

neck as he reversed our positions. His tongue was forceful, his teeth slightly uneven, and his breath sweet. No smoker, obviously.

We were both breathing heavily when we came out of that clinch. By that time my overalls had become unzipped, I don't know how or when. He unfastened my bra. I was frantic to get it off and to release my arms from the overalls He ran his finger round my nipples, though they hardly needed touching to become erect. I got the zip of his overalls down and tried pushing my fingers through the curly mat on his chest. He bent over my breasts, and I shivered, remembering Toby's attack. He put my hands aside, holding my eye with his. He looked determined, even a little grim. I closed my eyes, and told myself that I knew Hob wouldn't hurt me. He didn't. He kept his hands moving, he kissed me in more places than I've ever been kissed before, but he never once hurt me.

He pushed down on my overalls, and I eased them from under my hips. I wanted him to take me, for all sorts of reasons, some good and some bad. He pulled the blanket straight under my thighs, and I stiffened, in spite of myself. He was stroking my legs at the time. He looked up, still stroking, as if to ask whether I really meant him to to take me all the way. I stared back, leaving the decision to him. He waited for me to make up my mind.

'Is there something I ought to say, or do?' I

asked.

He shook his head, smiling as one might smile at a child.

'Please!' I said, but he had decided against it. He lay down, close to me, and held me in his arms. We were to kiss and cuddle, but not to take matters any further. I could feel he was ready for it, and I tried to convince him that I was, too, but apparently he'd made up his mind not to take me, and that was that. The bed springs protested; they'd probably been doing so for some time, only I hadn't noticed.

'What's that?' mumbled a male voice from next door. Toby.

Rose muttered something about 'damned cocks' and 'far too early'.

I started to giggle. Hob put his mouth over mine to keep me quiet. I could feel him shake with laughter, as well. The more I laughed, the more he shook. We struggled for composure, holding each other tightly, warm body against warm body, and the inevitable happened. As Hob slid into me, I gave a muffled shriek. He gripped the back of my neck and held me even more closely while I panted, absorbing pain. He kept rigidly still, not moving. I breathed deeply, and with each breath felt him enter me further. The pain was unendurable at first . . . then bearable . . . and then it was merely uncomfortable to have him there. We were true Siamese twins now, I thought.

Instead of thrusting him away, I tightened

118

my arms round him We lay entwined, warm and damp. My face was clammy; he kissed me gently, reassuringly. And did not withdraw.

The bed next door creaked, and I wondered what I would do if Toby chose to come in to us at that moment. I gasped, and involuntarily let Hob deeper in. I found I was crying, but whether I cried from joy or pain, I couldn't have said. He seemed to understand. His fingers soothed me, kept me still. I began to feel very excited. I wanted . . . something more, but I didn't know how to get it. Hob wouldn't allow me to go on any longer, but carefully withdrew from me, doing his best not to hurt me any more. He mopped up between my legs and lifted the stained blanket to show me, before throwing it under the bed. I didn't particularly want to bother resuming my overalls again, because I felt so lazy, but he seemed to think I should, so I did so. I'm not sure I even said 'Thank-you' to him before I fell asleep again.

*   *   *

'Delightful!' said a sneering voice above me. 'Babes in the Wood, eh? May you sleep as soundly tonight.'

It was Toby, of course. I blinked myself awake, to find that Hob and I had managed to become almost as closely entwined in sleep as we had done when we had made love. Hob was awake, smiling foolishly into the sunlight. Of course, he always pretended to be mentally deficient when Toby was around. I don't know what time it was, but it was later than I usually woke, for the sun was streaming into the room, and I seemed to remember that it usually only did that about nine o'clock. My watch had stopped. Toby stood at the window and gazed out; he must have drawn the curtain back when he first came in. He was fully dressed.

Toby let Hob go to the bathroom, and then clipped his ankle to the bed once more, saying that Hob was less trouble that way; he could be set free after I'd got rid of Mr. Brent's men. I tried to catch Hob's eye, but he wasn't playing.

'I must wear my own clothes when they come,' I protested. 'They mustn't see me like this when they come to fetch the hens, or they'll suspect something.' It seemed to me that I'd had the germ of an idea about escaping when I woke up, but I needed time to winkle it out and work on it.

Toby was unexpectedly genial. He said I might change, and then come down to cook breakfast for them all. He said Sid could come and sit in the little room with Hob, armed with the truncheon. One squeak or wrong move out of Hob, and Sid would knock him for six. I didn't think that was very funny.

My own clothes were in the big bedroom. Rose was still there, making herself up in leisurely fashion. I washed and dressed, thinking hard. My plan wasn't perfect, but it might work, and it was the only one I had. It seemed to me that Rose was the weak link in Toby's chain, not only because he felt it best to keep her in ignorance of the murders he had committed, but also because she thought a lot of her creature comforts. She was bleary-eyed this morning, and slow. I hoped she was awake enough to understand what I said.

'You got away without any trouble yesterday?' I asked.

She nodded. 'Lots of cops. One of them had bright red hair. I quite liked the look of him.'

'They won't look back through their records and point the finger at you later? That bearded fellow who was organising things at the Office—he wouldn't be able to give them your address?'

'Who, Pete? He hasn't got it. Or rather, he's got an address I gave the Agency ages ago, but I've moved from there since. I was only there a week, you know. Just to give me an address in a good part of London. Anyway, I didn't have much to do with him . . . saw more of his wife . . . she did the letters and he did the talking. Nice girl. She's expecting, you know. I used to tell her she'd give herself a miscarriage, tripping over her skirts.' A shadow passed over her face. 'I did give her my telephone number once . . .' She brightened. 'But she'll never have kept it. She's got dozens of scraps of paper in her pockets with important messages on them, and she's always losing them. And I'm not going back to my digs so what does it matter, anyway?'

So she still didn't know that Pete and his wife were dead. I feared Toby might have told her last night in bed, but he hadn't. So far so good.

'About tonight,' I said. 'Toby said you are going to spend the night sitting up in an Airport Lounge. It sounds as if it might be uncomfortable.' She grimaced; she agreed, but didn't see any help for it. 'I could help you there,' I suggested. 'I share a flat with another girl in South Kensington. I could put you all up for the night, if I can get rid of my flatmate. It would be a lot safer for you, and more comfortable.'

'But Toby said you weren't co-operating, and we'd have to leave you here when we went. He said I'm to ring through to Mr. Brent when we're ready to go into the Departure Lounge tomorrow.'

'I've changed my mind about not co-operating. After all, I did drive the van yesterday, so I'm in with you whether I like it or not. Also Toby said I could have five hundred pounds out of this, so I might as well pull my weight and see that you get away safely. If you got caught, you'd split on me, wouldn't you? I think you're taking an unnecessary risk hanging around in the open at the Airport all night. Much better if you stay with me quietly until it is time to go. You could go direct to the Air Terminal from my flat, because it's only a couple of hundred yards away. I suppose I could even drive you there, to save you carrying the luggage.'

She applied lipstick with a brush. 'It's an idea,' she admitted. 'I'll speak to Toby about it. I'll look a wreck if I have to stay up all night.'

So far, so good.

I went downstairs and cooked breakfast. Sid refused to eat his upstairs on a tray. He said it was ridiculous to stand guard on Hob when he was manacled to the bed. Toby shrugged, and agreed, so I took a laden tray upstairs for myself and Hob. He lay with one leg stretched out in front of him, and swung the other. He had been trying to do something about the bandages on his feet, so I fetched a bowl of water and tore the pillowcase into strips to make him more comfortable. I found I didn't particularly wish to look him in the eye, so I talked and ate with my head down, bringing him up to date on my plan. I felt full of energy, but uneasy. I had pushed my feet into a pair of bedroom slippers; my feet weren't too bad, considering. Nothing like as bad as Hob's were.

Beneath us we could hear the rumble of men's voices, with Rose's sharp, high tones overriding them now and then. I kept my own voice low. There were plenty of weak places in my plan, but it might buy us time, and get us out of the house and back to London; once within screaming reach of other people, we would have more opportunities to escape.

I stationed myself at the window and looked over the courtyard and along the lane which led to the outside world. The hens clacked and strutted over the pile of debris from the house. I studied the sky; it was misty and promised another hot day. I studied the dark, lush green of the trees behind the shed. I studied the yard, cobble by cobble. I didn't want to look at Hob. I knew him and yet did not know him.

I felt I'd been over-emotional about him, and now I wondered whether I'd gone too far. I didn't exactly regret what had happened between us, but I would have felt happier if we hadn't had to meet again. I felt confused. It was possible that I'd been romanticising about him . . . we'd been thrown together under unusual circumstances . . . he'd been kind . . . maybe I'd been making a fool of myself over him too.

I kept my back to him for a long time, and then risked a peep over my shoulder. His eyes were on the wall beside me, but he didn't see it. He was thinking, one hand combing through his curls, the other relaxed across the rail at the top of the bed. I tried to view him dispassionately, and found I was going back to my old argument that I couldn't get involved with him because he was a tramp; whereas I knew perfectly well that he wasn't.

I wondered if he had made a good teacher, and decided he probably had, because he had an air of decision about him when Toby was not around. Now I came to study him closely, he looked every inch the professional than in holiday clothes.

I decided I was indulging in yet more wishful thinking, and returned my eyes to the yard.

'Sarah!' That was Toby yelling for me to do the washing up. I didn't look at Hob as I picked up our tray and yelled back that I was coming. Passing through the big bedroom, I saw that Rose had left the slacks she had worn the day before, in a heap on the floor. I remembered how she had torn a strip of newspaper off, and thrust it into her pocket. Of course, that little incident had nothing to do with us . . . had it?

I put the tray down, and examined her slacks. The scrap of newspaper wasn't there.

Downstairs, the atmosphere was tense. Sid was scowling. Rose was fiddling with a cigarette, a bright spot of natural colour on either cheek upsetting the balance of her makeup. Toby was excitedly striding about, hands in pockets.

'Up!' he said to Sid, when he saw me 'Sit with Hob, and if he tries to signal for help, let him have it with the truncheon. And don't come down until I yell that it's all clear.'

I cleared the table, trying to look innocent.

125

'Tell him about your flat, Sarah!' said Rose. 'I've been trying to tell him about it, but he . . .'

'I don't want to hear any more about her flat!'

Rose slapped a couple of plates together and put them on my tray. She was furious. I could see Toby's dilemma; he didn't want to tell Rose why he couldn't trust me to house them up in London, and yet he could see the advantage of spending his last night in England so close to the Air Terminal. He couldn't be sure that I'd overheard him planning to kill me, and yet he thought I probably knew I was doomed. He didn't want Rose to be angry with him, and yet he couldn't disillusion her.

I said, 'We've got two single beds in our bedroom, and we have a camp bed we can put up in the living-room. Also there's a sofa. My flat-mate sometimes stays overnight with her boyfriend, and there's no reason why I shouldn't ring her before we leave here . . . from the call-box down the road . . . she wouldn't mind, I'm sure, if I suggested she let me have the flat to myself tonight. There's no porter, or anything like that. No one need see you.'

'And I don't fancy a night spent sitting upright at the Airport,' said Rose.

'It could be a trap,' said Toby.

'No trap!' I assured him. 'You were going to give me some money so that I could have

126

a good holiday abroad, weren't you? Well, I'll do just that. We'll all go to the Airport early tomorrow morning. Hob and I will catch the first plane out—it doesn't matter where it goes to. You can see us off, and then catch your own plane.'

'Radio links. You could contact the police via the pilot.'

Rose gave me a bright smile. 'Or we could always leave them tied up in her flat, Toby . . . Why not? That was your original plan for her, wasn't it? Her flat-mate would find her when she got back from work, so she wouldn't come to any harm.'

'I'll think about it,' said Toby.

'Thank you,' I said.

'Thank you, darling,' said Rose, and kissed him. She was all smiles, helping me wash up. I wasn't. I thought Toby had given in too easily, and feared he'd thought up some plan to counter mine. He couldn't allow us to live, could he?

As I put the last of the pans back into place, Mr. Brent's truck came trundling down the lane. He'd come himself, with one of his men, and two young lads—the sons of his head cow-man—who were on holiday. I went out, with Toby whom I introduced to him. Rose stayed indoors, out of sight. I had to apologise for having allowed the hens to run free, but as I hadn't fed them that morning, they were comparatively easy to catch. Toby volunteered

127

to help, and stuck so close to me that I had no chance to speak to any of our visitors privately. In fact, I didn't dare try, for as we went to fetch some grain he muttered in my ear that Sid had orders to strangle Hob if I gave the game away.

We rounded up most of the hens with ease, but one or two were annoyingly evasive, and we had to hunt them all over the place. At one point I tripped over the rubbish in the middle of the yard, but luckily I fell on something soft—the suit Hob had worn when he arrived. A patched trouser leg lay uppermost. The original tweed suit must have been a good one; a fine dog-tooth pattern of brown and green. The patch was of a different, a rust brown. I remembered both tweeds well; I remembered my grandfather wearing that suit, and the patch had been taken from a pleated skirt my grandmother had made for me when I was a child. Hob had stumbled into my life wearing a cast-off suit of my grandfather's.

I staggered to my feet, reeling. One of the boys asked me whether I'd hurt myself. I shook my head.

'That the old scarecrow suit?' he asked. 'Saw he'd lost it, the other morning. Going to let us have it back, then?'

I held it out to him, and looked around for Toby. Luckily he was involved with Mr. Brent, discussing the finer points of Range Rovers, or some such mechanical matter. The scarecrow.

128

Of course! Grandfather had let Mr. Brent have his old suit for the scarecrow which stood in the lower field, the field which bordered the road along which Hob must have come. Hob had been walking along the road when Toby had come haring along in my Mini, and knocked him down.

So far so good.

So what had Hob been wearing when Toby knocked him down?

CHAPTER FOUR

Toby put his arm round me as I waved goodbye to the Brent truck, and my hens. He had called me 'Darling' several times while the visitors had been around, and had kept up the pretence of being my boyfriend very well.

I shook his arm off as our visitors rounded the bend in the lane.

'Naughty!' said Toby, and laughed.

'If you try to touch me again I'll tell Rose.'

His face hardened, but I didn't follow up my advantage. I wanted time to think before I spoke to him again, and above all, I wanted to find the scrap of paper which Rose had pocketed last night behind Toby's back. I remembered how the and Sid had kept looking at it, and then at us, comparing . . . what?

'Coffee!' he said 'And then we'll trot along

to the phone box and ring your flat-mate, all right?' He cupped his hands and yelled to Sid to come down.

I went inside, and put the kettle on. Sid plodded down the stairs and went outside, where he and Toby began to transfer the money from the van back into the house. Rose was nowhere to be seen—probably upstairs; yes, I could hear bath water running. She had left her handbag on the table, so I waited till Toby and Sid were in the yard before snatching it up and retreating with it to the kitchen. Rose was untidy; lipsticks, eyebrow pencils, used tissues, were all jumbled together in the bottom of her bag, together with stubs of tickets, a greasy film of powder . . . Ugh! In side pockets she had a lot of papers, including her driving licence, but no newspaper cutting. I slammed the bag down, annoyed. Her powder compact flew open, and there it was, carefully folded into four.

I smoothed it out, to see a head and shoulders snap of Hob, dressed in collar and tie, with hair and beard neatly trimmed.

'"Brilliant Young Archaeologist Disappears"' I read. "The car and clothes of Mr. James Denison, one of our foremost authorities on Roman Britain, were found early yesterday morning in mysterious circumstances. Mr. Denison, a lecturer at South Bank University, had been spending a sailing holiday with friends in Sussex, and was due to arrive in York today to advise on the preservation of some Roman remains recently uncovered on a building site. Instead, his car was discovered by a farm hand on the smooth green bank of a river in the very heart of the English countryside. It seems that Mr. Denison decided to take a midnight swim, and, unaware of the treacherous nature of the local waters, got into difficulties and drowned. His body has not yet been recovered. For Obituary Notice, see page . . ."'

Rose yelled down the stairs that she could do with some coffee, too. I suddenly realised that the kettle was boiling, and busied myself with cups and saucers.

So Hob was Mr. Brent's suicide! Or rather, the missing body.

I must stop calling him Hob; his name was James Denison, and he wasn't a tramp or a teacher, but a 'Brilliant Young Archaeologist'. I wondered if he really had lost his memory, and how he had come to fall foul of Toby.

I took coffee out to Toby and Sid, who were cleaning the van of fingerprints. Rose picked up her own cup and came out to join us, smelling of my talcum powder. They stood talking in the sunshine, while I stole back into the house and tore up the stairs.

He was sitting up, waiting for me.

I proffered the newspaper cutting. He read it, grinning, and then cleared his throat.

'So where's my Obituary?' he asked. 'I've a

fancy to read what people think of me now I'm supposed to be dead!'

*   *   *

He'd picked up a couple of hitch-hikers on his way up from the Coast, and because he was in no particular hurry, he had gone out of his way to put them down at their destination, which was the Festival site. Only then had he realised he was short of petrol. He'd started to look for a petrol station, but couldn't find one, and had finally run out about half a mile down the road from the turning off to Elm Tree House. Taking his petrol can, he had set out on foot to walk to the nearest garage. It had been dark by then and he was wearing dark clothes; a black sweater over grey slacks. The Mini had come recklessly fast round a bend and hit him, tossing him half over the hedge into the field. He remembered being hurtled through the air, and then, although this was not at all clear, he thinks he half fell and half staggered out of the hedge and pitched over onto his head. He blacked out. When he came to himself, he was shivering; he was stretched out on his back in a field. He sat up and was promptly sick, so he guessed he'd concussed himself in his fall.

But he couldn't understand why he'd been stripped; clothes, watch, wallet . . . even his shoes had disappeared. A half open gate stood near, leading onto the road, and beyond it he

132

could see the dimmed lights of a parked car. He got to his knees, intending to call for help. Another car swept along the road and in its headlights he saw that a big, fair-haired man was tossing a bundle of clothes into the back of the parked car. His clothes. But not his car. Hob guessed correctly that the fair-headed man had run him down, thought him dead, and was now about to dispose of the body. Hob couldn't guess what way or why—he wasn't thinking too clearly—but he could guess that it wouldn't do him any good to ask for help from the man who had run him down.

At this point I felt I had to add to Hob's story. 'Toby must have lost his nerve. He'd come down here to mastermind a raid, and on his way to telephone the man who was supposed to be driving him to the Festival site, he ran you down. He thought he'd killed you. He couldn't afford to draw attention to himself either by taking you to hospital, or calling the police, so he decided to stage an accident on the river bank. There are notices about the Angling Associations along that road, which he must have seen earlier, and of course the road follows the course of the river for a couple of miles on the way here. It was a brilliant piece of improvisation, I think!'

'Horrifying,' agreed Hob. He had a light, but pleasant voice. It had taken a minute or two for Hob to understand why Toby had stripped him, but when he did, he couldn't think what to do. His first thought was to get to the road and flag down another motorist, but Toby stood between him and the road. Then Toby turned and came back into the field, presumably intending to collect one very dead body. The moment when the two men had come face to face must have been shattering for Toby.

'And for me,' said Hob, grinning sourly. 'After the first moment of shock, I could see he was furious with me for being alive. He picked up a biggish stone that was propping the gate open, and came after me with it. A whole fleet of cars was passing by on the road at that moment, but they were less than no help, for they gave him enough light to see me by and remember that by that time I was half naked . . . I thought I could maybe dodge around and get back to the road somewhere else. I started to run away from the road and the headlights . . . I couldn't run very fast, partly because I was still feeling groggy, and partly because I had no shoes on. On the other hand, once I was away from the road, it was very dark, and he couldn't see as well as I. I came to another hedge, and got through it . . . I could hear him coming after me . . . I knew I wouldn't last long in the open, especially if the moon should . . . There was a ditch. I rolled into it, and tried to camouflage myself with mud and leaves. It wasn't deep, but there were one or two places where there was more cover than others. It seemed to me I must be visible for miles but I could hear him blundering about, even shouting for me . . . He went back to the car once, and I thought he'd gone. The moon was bright at the time . . . shifting clouds . . . you know? I daren't risk moving. The field was a big one, with no cover in it. He came back, trying to move softly, but I heard him He had a stick with him, and he beat at the hedge with it, frightened the wild life; but he missed me. He passed by on the other side of the hedge. I could hear him cursing. Then he changed his tactics and called out that he meant me no harm, that he wanted to take me to hospital. I remembered how he'd stripped me, and gone for me with a stone, and I stayed where I was. At last I heard him start up his car and drive off. By that time I was in a bad way. In theory I could go back to the road and flag down the next car, but I simply hadn't the nerve to do so. I couldn't remember what car my assailant had been driving—I'd only seen it for a flashing second in the headlights of another car—and I was scared I might step out and flag down not a friend, but the very man who had attacked me. It seemed to me only reasonable that he'd anticipate that I would go back to the road. All he would have to do to pick me up, would be to patrol that stretch of road until I saw fit to return to it. Then I remembered my car; it wasn't far off, and if I could find it, there was an old pair of trousers in the boot, and my briefcase in the back . . . with clothes and some evidence of identification, I could cope. But I couldn't find my car. I must have gone the wrong way, I suppose, because although I was making my way along the road on the field side of the hedge, and I thought I'd left it only about a hundred yards along . . .'

'Toby took it. He must have cruised along, as you said he would, until he came to an abandoned car. He'd check your wallet with the identification in the briefcase, realise the car belonged to you, and take it to the river bank, with your clothes, to stage your "suicide".'

'I ought to have seen his car then, but I didn't. I think that knock on the head . . . well, I found the scarecrow at last, and took his things . . . saw your light and thought I'd get help here. Only when I got here, everything was dark, and the house locked up. I did knock, but nobody heard. I was a bit half-hearted, I suppose. I felt like death. I know I blacked out at least once on the way. I got the door of the garage open a crack, and crawled in. I don't remember anything else until I heard your voice next morning, and stumbled out to see . . . him!'

'Did you recognise him straight away?'

'No, but I think I recognised him before he recognised me. We'd not seen each other clearly, you know, and maybe if I hadn't lost my nerve and run . . . I heard it in his voice, then. He knew who I was, and he knew that I knew, because I'd run. I thought he'd kill me there and then. When I came round, I despaired. Of all the bad luck, to run and run, and run back to him! When he questioned me, I didn't bother to reply. Maybe I'd been knocked on the head once too often, but I didn't seem able to feel fear, or anything. Fatalistically, I waited for him to finish me off. Now you must remember that he'd never heard me speak; I acted dumb out of sullenness and despair, but perhaps because he couldn't bring himself to kill me in front of you in cold blood, he made himself believe that I really was dumb. He accused me of being mentally deficient, of not being able to remember how I arrived here. I went along with his suggestion. Once started, I couldn't drop the masquerade without laying myself open to danger. So long as he could persuade himself that I was no threat to him, so long I might live—and no longer.'

'You could have told me.'

'I thought you were in it with him at first. The only time he left us alone together was on that first day when I was chained up and couldn't have run away even if I had spoken. After that, when I began to understand that you'd been conned, too . . .' I went a painful red, but he merely smiled and touched my cheek, '. . . it was too late. If you come to think about it, we haven't been given any opportunity until now to foregather and talk without their overhearing us.'

We both glanced over to the window. It was shut, in spite of the warm weather, but we could faintly hear the voices of the three conspirators in the yard.

'Even last night,' said Hob. 'I had decided to talk to you, but when every word they spoke next door could be heard by us, it didn't seem to be a very good idea to break my silence. If we could have got free, and squeezed out of the window, then perhaps it might have been worth a try.'

'This is the smallest window in the house,' I said absently. 'Besides, Toby has all the car keys, and we could never make it to the road without transport . . . at least, I might if I could find a decent pair of shoes, but you never could.' I told him what I planned, and he approved. He said he'd been racking his brains for an alternate plan, but hadn't managed to come up with anything foolproof.

'You're so calm about it,' I said. Somehow we were holding hands, which made it easier to talk to him 'Aren't you afraid?'

'I'm tired. The shock of that night when he hunted me through the fields seems to have numbed me. Then the horror of watching that candle burning down . . . refuse to let myself panic again. I've had a good life, and done most of the things I wanted to do . . .'

'Don't be so apathetic!' I cried. 'Don't you want to live?'

'I'm tired,' he repeated. 'My head aches. I want to rest . . . there's nothing I can do.'

I kissed him.

'Don't!' he said, but not as if he meant it. 'Don't wake me up again, Sarah. I've only just reasoned myself into a state of acceptance . . .'

'Do I call you "James"?'

'Go on calling me "Hob". I like it, and it would be safer.'

'Your wife?'

'A long time dead. And I've been a long time lonely.'

'Am I like her?'

'A little. They say men usually repeat their mistakes, don't they?'

'It would be a mistake to get involved with me?'

'A figure of speech. We were happy enough until she became ill.'

'I'm very healthy,' I said, and then was furious with myself for being so gauche.

He smiled. 'And you can cook, and keep house, and you're a terrible scold!'

'I'm not good with men,' I said, trying to be honest with him.

'You will be,' he assured me, meaning something else.

'I will? I never thanked you for last night.'

'It is I who should thank you. That was only the beginning, for you. If I could only show

139

you . . .'

'I thought there was more to it, than that!'

He started to laugh, and I stifled the sound with my hand over his mouth. He took my hand away from his mouth and reached for me. He didn't look tired or resigned to his fate now. I thought that I ought to tell him not to, because we were wasting time. But somehow I didn't.

*   *   *

Rose was counting money into four piles; one big pile each for Toby, Sid and Rose, and one small pile for me. We watched in silence. Hob had been left upstairs, handcuffed to the bed, smiling sleepily into the sun.

'All right?' Toby asked. No one replied. 'Then I'll take Sarah along the road to make her phone call. No-one is likely to come here in our absence, are they?'

'The furniture dealer will come back sometime, but not until I contact him. I told my mother I'd ring her sometime yesterday or today, though.'

'And this phone is out of order. So she'll ring up to check, and maybe send an engineer along to put the fault right. Well, Rose and Sid had better stay indoors and keep the front door locked while we're gone. That way, if anyone comes down the lane they'll think you're out shopping, and they'll go away again.

All right, Rose?'

'I'll pack and clean up here while you're gone.'

Sid pocketed his pile. 'I could leave ahead of you. I'd like to take the quieter roads in Rose's car, and not risk the main roads.'

'We all leave together,' said Toby. 'And just to make sure that we do, I'll take Rose's keys with me.'

I tried not to look upset when Rose went to her handbag, because I still had the newspaper cutting in my pocket. Luckily she didn't check her powder compact. Come to think of it, she wouldn't have risked his seeing she'd disobeyed him and kept a cutting from the newspaper. She handed him her keys in silence. Sid looked sullen, but resigned. I intended to put the cutting back into her handbag, but I didn't have a chance before I left with Toby.

We drove in my Mini. Toby wasn't in the mood for conversation, and neither was I. The nearest phone booth was a good mile off; I dialled my flat-mate's number at work, and spoke to her with Toby glued to my side. I had considered trying to hint to her that I was in trouble, but when I saw Toby's hand hover over the receiver, ready to cut me off, I decided against it. I made the call brief. I was coming back to London that night—yes, it was early, but some friends of mine . . . no, no-one she knew . . . they wanted to come up with me, stay overnight, and take me out to a show and all that. Would the place be free so that they could stay the night? My flat-mate sounded amused, because she was aware how many times I'd been pressed to take a boyfriend in for the night, and had refused to do so. She thought I'd succumbed to Toby's charm at last, and she couldn't resist twitting me about him. I gritted my teeth, remembering how I'd bored her with talk of Toby before I'd left London. She said she'd be delighted to advance the cause of my romance with Toby, and that I wouldn't see hide or hair of her that night. I said thanks, and rang off.

'Good girl!' applauded Toby. We eyed each other. I knew for certain at that moment that he still meant to kill me. His eyes were impersonal. I was no longer a living, breathing and desirable woman to him, but a lay figure whose presence he found inconvenient.

'I'll tell Rose!' The phone booth was stuffy and smelt of dirt.

'What will you tell her?'

'About Hob—James Denison' I pulled the cutting from my pocket and showed it to him. —' You tried to kill him. Rose doesn't know that, does she?'

'Nonsense!' But his eyes changed direction. He grabbed my wrist and wrenched the cutting out of my fingers. He tore it across, once, twice, and let the scraps flutter to the floor.

'She doesn't know you're a murderer,' I

said, firing all my guns at once. 'She doesn't know what happened in the wood. I've heard her speak of Pete and his wife with affection. I don't think she'd like to think of you as a murderer, or of herself as an accessory.'

His eyes moved from me to consider his reflection in the mirror above the phone. It was cracked, but it assured him he still looked the same.

'You'd better be careful,' I warned him. 'You'd better let Hob and me take a plane before you. We won't talk I can promise you that. We're accessories, just as much as Rose and Sid. But the moment you try to kill us, I'll tell Rose, and you'll lose her.'

I pushed open the heavy door of the phone booth and swallowed fresh air. He followed me out and actually held open the door of the Mini for me to climb into the passenger seat.

'What's that?' I asked, seeing a car radio on the back seat. 'Is that yours?'

'That's right. I didn't want Rose listening to News bulletins while we were away.'

I admired his foresight. If only he could keep newspapers away from Rose until they were in the air, he might even get away with it. I began to relax, because it looked as if my plans were going to work.

*   *   *

I'd reckoned without Rose's curiosity. In

our absence, she must have fiddled with the ancient radio at Elm Tree House, anxious to hear what coverage the media were giving to the robbery at the Festival. We could hear the boom of the radio as Toby and I drove into the yard, and then the sound was turned down, adjusted to normal hearing. I glanced at Toby's watch, as he was doing; it was just on half past eleven, and time for a news summary. Toby understood, and was out of the car with a gasp and a curse. I followed, because even in his haste he remembered to take the ignition key with him.

'. . . the second victim is still in the Intensive Care Unit, but has been able to give the police the following description of one of the men who attacked her and murdered her husband. About five foot six in height, slender build, short dark hair, brown complexion, brown eyes. No noticeable scars. The other two men are tall and well-built. The police say that these men are dangerous and that members of the public should not approach them under any circumstances . . .'

Toby pulled the cord out of the socket and sent the radio sprawling onto the floor in a crash of broken parts. Sid had been out in the garage, and was now standing in the doorway behind me, with a stupid, fearful look on his face. Although the radio usually refused to produce any sound for me, it had obeyed Rose's fingers . . . and destroyed us.

She stood at the end of the table with her hands over her mouth. Her eyes were on Toby, horrified, and yet knowing. I thought she might well be sick. She looked at Toby for a long time, as if trying to readjust her mental picture of him, and then she looked past him at me.

I could see her going over my description to herself, 'five foot six, slender build . . .' Pete might be dead and unable to talk, but his wife was still alive and she had taken a good look at me when I had stripped off my helmet and scarf in the wood yesterday. She would know me again.

'They don't know she's a girl,' said Toby. 'Not yet, anyway.'

Rose made the shape of 'no' with her mouth, but no sounds came out. She transferred her hands to her neck, holding herself together.

'Shock!' I said. 'Shall I get her a stiff drink?' I didn't wait for permission, but made straight for the kitchen. Hob and I hadn't wasted our precious time together that morning, and while I had made sure that he received satisfaction the second time round, he had told me how I might cheat death, if I were allowed enough time to prepare . . .

'Sarah!' yelled Toby. I dropped everything and ran back with a glass of sloe gin. Toby took it off me and held it out to Rose. She woke out of her trance, screamed something unintelligible at him, and struck out at his arm. He caught her wrist and forced the glass to her teeth. She gagged, but drank.

My share of the robbery was now sitting behind Granny's souvenir mug from Eastbourne on the mantelpiece. Presumably it would be left there to tie me in with the robbery. Also the van. Sid was doing his bit in the yard by pouring paraffin onto my poor little Mini, and setting it alight.

I tried to creep back into the kitchen, but Toby caught sight of me, and gestured that I should go upstairs. 'Change back into your overalls, and don't forget your boots.'

I ran upstairs and into Hob's arms. I hardly needed to tell him what had happened, because he had heard most of it through the floor. I begged him to fight for his life, and he promised he would, whispering between hurried kisses. At least he was wide awake now. He asked me to pray for him if I were to live and he to die. I stood there with my hands in his, and couldn't think of anything appropriate to say in return.

'Sarah!' That was Toby, yelling from the bottom of the stairs.

'I'm changing!' I cried, and dived for my overalls and boots. My fingers were clumsy.

'Sarah!' Toby was coming up for me.

I ran into Hob, and gave him one last kiss.

'Here!' he breathed, thrusting something at me. 'Put it in one of your boots, rather than in a pocket—in case he searches you.'

It was a knife, a small sharp knife with an ivory handle whose edge had been whetted to a razor-sharp point. It was one of my grandfather's fruit knives, and I remembered that there had been two such knives in the box of cutlery and silver I had given Hob to clean on the morning he arrived. He must have taken one and hidden it against an emergency—and now he was giving it to me. I hesitated. He thrust it down inside my boot and turned from me before he could regret his generosity.

'Sarah!' Toby was in the doorway.

I choked on the word 'goodbye' and followed Toby downstairs. Rose was crying, but miserably rather than angrily. I knew Toby had persuaded her there was nothing for it but to cover their tracks with two more murders.

'Wash up the glass Rose has used,' Toby ordered. 'And wipe over the table and all the chairs. Rose, get your suitcase and see you haven't left any fingerprints upstairs. You've got our money safely packed?'

She sniffed and nodded her head at two carrier bags standing beside the door. I picked up the glass and went out to the kitchen. I could hear Sid and Toby talking. They were discussing which route each should take to get to London. Toby was telling Sid how to get to my flat, and searching my handbag for my keys. They would meet there, sleep there, and set off from there tomorrow morning for the Air Terminal.

Neat, but not gaudy, as my grandfather would have said.

My hands trembled so much that I dropped and broke the glass I was wiping. Toby came to the door and yelled at me to be careful.

'It doesn't matter now,' I said.

He thought that was hilariously funny. I wiped down the table in the living-room, and went over all the chairs. The fire had gone out, leaving the charred remains of the overalls and boots Toby had worn the day before. He made me pick them out of the ashes, and take them outside to bury in the flowerbed under my bedroom window.

I made one last bid for time.

'Mr. Brent knows about you. If they find us dead, but they don't find you, won't they switch the search to look for you?'

'Ah, but I won't be around, will I? I was just a visitor, passing through. Why should they look for me? It was your description which was broadcast, my poppet, not mine.'

That was unanswerable. Sid came out of the garage, holding up some tangles of rope and string.

'This what you want?' he asked.

I dropped the shovel with which I had been burying the remains of Toby's gear. Toby bade me replace it in the hearth and sweep it clean. I did so in a dream. The clock had stopped,

148

and so had my watch. I hadn't a clue what time it was.

I wondered if the furniture dealer would give my family a better price for the stuff from the house after today. 'Direct from Murder House, this fine oak sideboard . . .' It was a hideous piece of furniture really. I wiped it clean.

Rose came down the stairs, bleary-eyed, but otherwise her normal self. She avoided looking at me, which meant she'd written me off. She didn't look at Toby, either, as she waited for him to step aside from the door so that she could get out.

'That's right,' said Toby approvingly. 'No need for you to know anything about it. You go and sit outside in the sun, in my car, and I'll be with you in five minutes.'

She said something in a stifled voice about the keys. He laughed. She changed colour, and went off without them. Toby wouldn't risk letting her have the car keys until he was ready to drive off himself.

'I want to go to the bathroom,' I said.

'Is she feeling afraid, then?' he jeered.

I stumped up the stairs, and he followed me. I closed the bathroom door in his face and locked it. He thought that was very funny, too, and indeed from his point of view it was, for that particular door was only made of ply, and he could have broken it down with one shove of his shoulder.

149

I heard Sid follow us up the stairs. He spoke to Toby about the rope he'd brought with him. Would it be enough? Toby approved.

When I had my breathing under control, I unlocked the door and went out. Hob was already standing in the big bedroom, waiting for me. I stood aside to let him go into the bathroom, too. Toby and Sid both thought that funny, but I didn't. Hob had been secured to that bed for far too long. Hob didn't take long; perhaps he thought it was better to get it over with.

Toby ordered Hob to tie my wrists behind my back.

'No handcuffs?' asked Sid.

'I'd rather keep them on me,' said Toby. 'You never know when they might come in handy, and it would be a waste to use them on these two.'

Toby objected to the way Hob had tied my wrists at first, and made him do it again, more tightly.

'On the bed, Sarah!'

'Which bed?'

'This one will do.'

I climbed onto my grandparents' bed and lay down, facing the window. Hob was instructed to tie my ankles, above the heavy boots, so that I could not slip my feet loose.

'Not that it would matter, I suppose!' said Toby. 'Sid—you got the knife?'

Sid produced my grandmother's vegetable

knife. My mother had given it to her for a Christmas present.

'Pick your spot!' said Toby, grinning. Sid wiped the handle and blade and handed it to Hob, hilt foremost. Hob hesitated. Toby put one big hand round Hob's throat and squeezed. 'Pick your spot, little man. Anywhere from throat to stomach. Make sure she dies of it, that's all we ask.'

Hob got on the bed behind me. I looked up at him for a moment, and then turned away to lie in a foetal position on my left side. He bent over me, and with his left hand sought for my heart. He took his time over it, and then drove the knife in up to the hilt with his right hand. I heard him grunt with effort.

I coughed, twice. And jerked.

Toby came round the bed and stood between me and the window, darkening the room.

'Not bad!' I heard him murmur. 'Now take the knife out, man, so that we can see the damage.'

Hob's hand withdrew the knife slowly. I watched red liquid follow the blade and spread on the coverlet. I choked and dribbled.

'She's coughing blood all right,' said Sid. 'Taking the knife out always hurries things up.'

My eyes unfocused. They were dim against the light. I let my eyelids sink.

I heard them turn to leave the room, taking Hob down the stairs to die.

*   *   *

I waited with my eyes closed until I heard them shut and lock the front door. Then I sat up and started fishing with bound hands into my boot for the knife. I spat out the rest of the sloe gin I had been holding in my mouth since my visit to the bathroom, and ignored the smart of scraped skin on my upper arm. Acting on Hob's advice, I had used my minutes of freedom in the kitchen to raid my grandmother's store of home-made wines. I had poured some sloe gin into an empty medicine bottle to be sipped at the last possible moment, and the rest I had emptied into a plastic bag, and sealed it with tape. I had put both the medicine bottle and the bag of liquid into the baggy legs of my overalls, and slid the roll of tape and a pair of scissors into my pockets. Luckily Toby had not thought of searching me, and anyway, he wouldn't have thought the objects I was carrying in my pockets remarkable. Once in the bathroom, I had peeled off my overalls, and taped the sloshing, bulging bag of liquid to my skin over my heart. It was uncomfortable, but I couldn't risk it shifting, so I used a lot of tape. I wondered how Hob had kept the knife concealed for so long; the only article of clothing he'd kept on throughout his captivity had been his pants. Had he hidden the knife in them? It was possible, but not probable. He'd probably hidden it by slipping it between the bandages I'd put on his feet.

It was Hob who had thought of it; it was an actor's trick, he'd said, to slide a fake dagger between arm and breast, piercing a bag of red liquid so as to simulate the flow of blood. I had taken a swig of sloe gin before I'd left the bathroom, and emptied the rest of the bottle down the drain. Tape and scissors I'd dropped into the cistern, just in case.

Unfortunately Hob hadn't been able to use a fake dagger, and in spite of all his care, he'd driven the knife through the bag of liquid and into my skin. It was real blood that mingled with the sloe gin staining the coverlet as I struggled to reach his knife.

'It's up to you to fool them,' he'd said. 'Cough . . . jerk . . . go limp. Can you do it?'

'I'm sure I can, with my life at stake. But what about you?'

He didn't answer. He had worked out how I might be saved, but he didn't see how he could save himself, and I didn't, either.

I grasped the hilt of the knife and withdrew it from my boot. Turning it between my fingers, I started sawing on the rope round my wrists. Rose had opened the window sometime that morning, and Toby had forgotten to close it, so I could hear the preparations he and Sid were making in the yard.

'Yes, the beam should be all right,' yelled

Sid. He must be in the garage, looking up at the heavy oak beam that supported the roof. His voice sounded muffled. 'Should I move the van out?'

'I don't see why,' replied Toby. His voice came from directly beneath, and gave me a start. It reminded me that I must not make any sound, in my nightmare of effort, or he would realise I was not dead, and come back into the house to finish me off.

'It would give us more room,' said Sid. His voice was louder now. He was probably coming out of the shed. 'Shall I use some more of that rope to tie his wrists, before we string him up?'

'In front of him, perhaps,' said Toby. 'Suicides often do that, I believe, so as to prevent themselves from changing their minds half way through.' He laughed.

There was a scuffling sound, followed by a slap. Hob?

I sweated. I forced back a scream as the knife bit into my wrist. I wasn't much good at this. The heavy overalls hampered me; they were sodden all down my left side now, and the smell of gin was beginning to attract flies . . . and yes, there was a wasp!

'Idiot!' shouted Toby. 'Head him off from the lane!' I guessed that Hob was playing for time. Making a dash for freedom?

An angry yell from Sid, and the sound of a heavy blow. A sharp, thin clatter of metal thrown against stone. The knife? The knife with which Hob had 'killed' me? Sid was cursing over the sound of blows. Hadn't Hob been hit enough already?

I sobbed aloud, and then remembered Toby might hear me. The knife handle was slippery. I dropped it, and lost precious seconds groping for it on the rucked-up coverlet.

I could hear something, or somebody, being dragged across the yard. Hob was making it difficult for them. Or was he unconscious? Oh, God!

'Not that way,' said Toby, sharply. He sounded distant. Were they in the shed already? 'Hold him up for me, while I catch hold of the rope.'

'Hoist him on top of the van?'

'O.K. You lift him up to me, and I'll . . . yes, he could reach the beam from here, if he stretched. They'll not notice, anyway . . . not to an inch or two. Hand me up that far length of rope . . .'

I felt something give. A wrench. No, I hadn't done enough work on it yet.

'Keep still, you little brute!' That was Toby, again.

I tried to brush sweat from my forehead with my shoulder and discovered I was crying. This was no time for tears, I told myself.

'And . . . up . . . further! I've got him now!'

I had never hated anyone as I hated Toby.

'Aargh!' cried Sid.

'Did he kick you in the eye? For Christ's

155

sake, be careful!'

'Bloody . . .'

'Cursing him won't help. Tie his ankles . . . Keep still, you little devil, or I'll knock you out again!'

'It would be easier . . .'

'Too many bruises might look bad—ah you don't like the sight of the noose?'

With a convulsive jerk I freed my wrists. One was bleeding, but that couldn't be helped. The wasp buzzed around my head in an interested fashion, and I flailed at it. I flexed my fingers and set to work on the rope round my ankles. It wouldn't take long to free my legs, but I didn't see how I could help Hob, even if I did.

'All right?' That was Toby.

'Yup!'

Then I'll push him off when you let go his feet. Right?'

'Right!'

'One, two, three . . . go!'

A scrambling sound. Silence. I paused, my knife in mid-air. The wasp settled on the coverlet near my hand and started shambling in the sloe gin stain.

'All right?' Sid sounding dubious.

'I think so.' Toby didn't sound too pleased with himself, either. 'Maybe you should have pulled on his legs. He should have fallen clear and broken his neck . . .'

'You should have pushed him off.'

156

'I did, but he sort of slid down, instead of falling . . .'

He laughed, but in a sick way. 'He looks kind of funny . . . jerking and turning . . .'

'I'll finish him off. Pull on his legs.'

'N—no. The police might be able to tell that someone had interfered . . . it must look natural. No one can help him, so let him dance. He's kicked you and he's kicked me, so let him kick air for a change.'

They came out of the garage. I heard the grate of the door as they shut it, boxing Hob in with the stolen van.

I could imagine him dangling at the end of the rope, clutching at the rope round his neck perhaps . . .

'Here are the keys!' Toby must have tossed the keys of Rose's car to Sid. He dropped them, and swore. Toby laughed. I heard them walk round the side of the house to where their cars were parked.

I picked away at the rope round my ankles while yet another wasp homed in on me. There! I was free! I slid off the bed, clumsily, and stumbled into the wall. Suppose they had heard . . .!

No, the cars were being revved up, and driven into the yard. I inched to the side of the window, and risked a glance down. The two cars were stationary beneath me; Toby was half standing in his car, leaning out of the window and shouting at Sid. Why didn't they go? Please God, let them go quickly. My Mini was scarred with fire, and the closed doors of the garage stared at me reproachfully.

Toby got out of his car . . . Oh dear God, why the delay? . . . and went over to Sid, who was driving Rose's sports car. Sid was searching through his pockets. He got out of his car, too, and turned out his trouser pockets. He found something—something small—and handed it over to Toby.

'Oh no!' I breathed, as Toby pulled open one of the garage doors and went back in. I couldn't see into the garage from where I was, but Rose could, and so could Sid. Rose averted her lovely head and clasped her hands over her mouth, because whatever she had seen had made her feel ill. Sid shrugged, and got back into the sports car.

I leaned against the wall and mouthed prayers. I couldn't remember any more than the first line of Our Father, and it didn't seem to make sense the way I said it, but it helped to pass the awful seconds until Toby came out of the garage again.

I didn't move when I heard the door scrape shut. There was no point in my trying to get out of the house with the three of them looking on. The front door was locked, and the windows down below were all small. The window beside which I stood was my only hope; that, too, was small, but it lacked the central stone pillar which made the windows downstairs impossible. If I could only wriggle my hips through, I might be able to get out.

Sid drove off first, roaring down the lane. Toby said something to Rose which I didn't catch, and followed. I waited until I heard Toby change down for the bend in the lane, and then fought the window wide. Try as I would, I couldn't get my hips through.

'Fool!' I swore at myself, as I tore off overalls and boots. 'Wasting time!' I could have stripped while I was waiting for them to go. Clad in bra and pants, and striped with blood and sloe gin, I managed to get out of the window without taking more than inch of skin off my left shoulder-blade. Legs dangling, I hung onto the window ledge until I could gauge the distance to the ground. I hurt my ankle in the fall, but not badly enough to cripple me. It was lucky for me that they didn't build tall in the old days.

The trip across the yard was hard on my feet, and even harder on my nerves. Was Hob dead already? Surely he couldn't have survived . . . I forced the garage doors open, my hands clumsy with haste.

Hob slowly revolved at the end of a rope hanging from the central beam in the garage, his feet pointing to the floor, and his hands bound before him. His eyes were closed, and I didn't like the colour of his face.

I ran for his legs and tried to hold him up. The rope was so tight round his neck that it

159

didn't run loose when I eased the strain. He felt warm, but I couldn't tell if he were still alive or not.

I screamed. That was another waste of time and energy, but I was so desperate I couldn't think what to do. Clasping Hob's legs to me, I looked around for something to cut the rope, or something on which he might rest his weight. There didn't seem to be anything in reach, except the van.

He didn't weigh a lot, hanging at the end of the rope. His knees bent as I lifted them. I guided his body to the van, and opening the door I tried to step up inside, intending to hoist him back onto the roof. I wasn't tall enough, or strong enough. The ignition key had been thrown into the van and now lay on its seat. That was what Toby had taken off Sid at the last moment. The lack of the ignition key might have spoiled the picture which Toby had so carefully set up, and so he had delayed long enough to throw it into the van—just long enough to ensure Hob's death.

I tried to ease the rope away from his throat, but I couldn't take enough of his weight to pull it loose. It wasn't easy, balanced at an angle, holding Hob to me with one arm, and with the other trying to work the rope loose. I wished I'd had the sense to bring my knife with me. What had happened to the knife with which Hob had 'killed' me? Had I heard it clatter on the cobbles in the yard when he made his bid to escape? If so, it might still be somewhere in the yard, because Toby couldn't risk carrying it away with him.

I fed Hob's legs through the window of the van, so that he could rest some of his weight by sitting on the sill, and climbed down to look for the knife. I was crying again, and cursing and praying, all in a jumble. Was I doing the wrong thing by leaving him, even to fetch the knife? Was I killing him, or was he already dead and all my trouble in vain?

I found the knife just outside the garage door, and ran back with it. Was it my imagination, or did his body jerk as I scrambled into the cab? I attacked the rope, trying to hold his shoulders towards me, so that he should not fall to the ground when the rope parted. There! Had he moved? Had I imagined it? I sawed at the rope frantically until it parted, and he half fell and half slipped into the cab with me clutching at his overalls. I got the noose off, and tried to suppress the thought that surely no-one could live with such indentations on their throat . . . calling his name rubbing his throat, and wondering whether it was the right thing to do . . . trying to remember First Aid . . . trying to feel for his heart . . . I couldn't tell whether he was alive or dead, and the phone was cut, even if I could scramble back inside . . .

Did his eyelids flicker? Had he moaned, and had I covered the tiny sounds of recovering consciousness with all the noise I'd been making? Should I try artificial respiration? I bent my head to try, and his eyes flicked open. Feebly he drew back his head to gasp for air. His hands were still bound. I helped him sit upright, trying to breathe deeply with him, feeling the effort hurt me as it hurt him. When he bent forward to put his head between his knees, I thought he had fainted, and started to howl. He put his hands on my thigh and left them there.

My body began to make reports to my brain that I'd misused it; my ankle hurt like blazes, as did my shoulder, and the knife slit on my arm. I drew the back of my hand across my face and sniffed, wondering if I dared look in the driving mirror. I decided I'd rather have a wash, first.

Hob raised his head and hoarsely mouthed the word 'Water'. His voice had gone, but no sound in the world could have been sweeter to me at that moment than that rough gasp for help. He was so exhausted he found it hard to move. I found out later what had happened. As soon as he'd been left alone, he'd tried to swing his body up onto the roof of the van. He'd failed, and lost consciousness about the time I got to him. But since he had managed to slip off the roof of the van, and not fallen, he had taken the strain of the rope round his neck gradually, and not in a jerk, so that he had never been in danger of breaking his neck, only of strangulation.

I told him to stay where he was and rest, while I went for some water. He nodded. Even as I wriggled down from the cab, I wondered how I was going to find water for him, with the house shut up, and how—belated thought—I was to contact the police.

Pushing the garage door wide open, I froze, for a car was coming down the lane. Reversing, making angry, impatient bursts of sound. The back of Toby's car came into view, with Rose sitting twisted around in the passenger seat, and Toby glancing around now and then to adjust his steering. Behind him I glimpsed the sports car, with Sid's heavy head twisted back on his shoulder.

For a moment I couldn't move. We were in no condition to resist them now. All our effort gone for nothing . . . I slumped against the door, defeated.

A scratching sound. Hob was trying to get out of the van. He had heard the cars, too.

'They're coming back,' I said. 'We've had it.'

He made croaking sounds, gesturing to the back of the garage with one hand over his throat, massaging it. I looked, and stiffened. Two pitchforks, ancient but serviceable, leaned against the back wall in a muddle of garden implements.

If we dragged one of the garage doors closed, and shot the bolts into the roof beam and the ground, then we would only have a narrow opening to defend. No matter that our defence could only last a little while. It was sufficient for the moment that the next step was clear.

I secured the one door, and pulled the other almost shut. I thought Rose had already seen me, but I needed time to help Hob, who was struggling to get the pitchforks out, and making heavy weather of it. One out . . . two. Hob looked awful. He couldn't stand upright without leaning on something. I wanted that 'something' to be me, but for the moment he had to make do with the van. The van? Could we get away if we drove out of the garage in the van? No, they were between us and the lane, and they were three fit people to two convalescents.

Why had they returned?

Pitchfork at the ready, I peered out.

Rose and Toby were getting out of their car, looking belligerent; or rather, Toby looked belligerent, while Rose looked as if she were going to cry. Sid slid the sports car back into line with theirs. He was shouting, but I couldn't make out the words above the racket of the tractor which was pressing them back into the yard.

The tractor! I eased my door open a little more, and saw Mr. Brent in the driving seat of his biggest tractor, pressing the bumper of the sports car back and back. Hitched behind the tractor was a half-filled wagon piled

164

with bales of hay, and standing on the hay was Mr. Brent's head cow-man, with a shotgun pointing at Toby's midriff. Two of his farmhands clung to the back of the wagon, and running behind them down the lane came the two lads who had helped round up the hens that morning.

'Sarah!' bellowed Mr. Brent. 'Are you all right?'

I pushed the door open, and emerged, pitchfork in hand.

'My dear girl!' His jaw dropped, and he killed the engine. He looked shocked, as did everyone else.

'I'm all right really,' I said, realising that to their eyes I must appear to be covered in blood. 'Most of it's sloe gin, although I have hurt my ankle and . . .' I swallowed, thinking I couldn't afford to dissolve into tears again. 'Hob's in a bad way, though. Can you get a doctor for him?'

Toby shouted something . . . I really think he went out of his mind for a moment as he realised that not only was I alive, but that he'd failed to kill Hob as well. He lunged for me, and I stood there, stupidly gaping at him, quite unable to defend myself. Hob did it for me. His pitchfork snaked over my shoulder and held Toby off. I could see that Hob could hardly hold it straight from exhaustion, but neither Toby nor I could miss the determination in his eye; if Toby touched me,

165

he was a dead man.

Rose screamed. 'No more killing!' she wailed.

'Who's been killed, then?' demanded Mr. Brent.

'Pete and his wife,' I said. 'Tell them, Toby. Tell Mr. Brent all about it.'

He said nothing, but his eyes went from me to the tines of the pitchfork and back.

'I'll tell,' said Rose, her voice breaking. 'I can't . . . Oh, why did I say I'd come?'

Toby turned on her. He knocked her flying, and ran for the lane. He didn't get far, but disappeared under a flurry of arms and legs as Mr. Brent's men jumped on him.

'And this?' Mr. Brent pointed at Hob, whose weary arms had dropped the pitchfork as soon as the moment of danger had passed. Hob sagged. I caught him as he fell, and knelt beside him.

'He's not one of them,' I explained. 'His name is James Denison, the man you thought had been drowned in the river. Toby ran him down on the road while he was walking along to get some petrol for his car. He ran away when Toby tried to kill him, and fortunately for me, he made his way back up here. I sort of . . . got fond of him, I suppose. Toby made me drive the van yesterday by threatening to burn James to death. He's saved my life today, and nearly lost his own . . . won't you fetch the doctor?'

166

*   *   *

I'll never say a word against hens for the rest
of my life, for it was they who had saved us.
To Toby's mind I had behaved perfectly when
the Brent people had come to collect the hens,
but in the eyes of one who had known me from
childhood, I had been behaving strangely.
For instance, I had been staying with my
grandparents at holiday times for years, and I
was as familiar with the hens' routine as with
that of my grandparents'—yet the hens had
not been shut up the previous night, ready for
collection. My explanation on that point hadn't
rung true.

Mr. Brent had been pardonably annoyed at
having to waste time chasing hens all over the
place when he was busy hay-making. At first
he had tried to be charitable, thinking my sin
of omission must be due to the presence of my
lover, but the closer he observed us, the less
natural did my manner appear. I jumped when
Toby addressed me as 'Darling', and there had
been a bruise on my arm which had not been
there the day before. Also I was limping, and
wearing bedroom slippers, instead of the boots
which would have been more appropriate wear
for the task of rounding up hens.

Again, why was my treasured Mini sitting in
the yard, and not tucked up under cover in the
garage? And why were the doors of the garage

closed, if it was empty? Mr. Brent puzzled over these points, and perhaps even more over my failure to invite him and his men in for a celebratory drink of home-made wine or coffee after the hens had been gathered in.

On their way back to the farm, one of the young lads had told Mr. Brent that there were two smashing cars hidden round the back of the house, out of sight of the yard.

One car Mr. Brent could understand; that could have been Toby's. But . . . two cars?

The district was shaking with talk of the murder and the raid on the Festival. It was only natural that Mr. Brent should begin to wonder if the events were in any way connected with the odd goings-on at Elm Tree House.

He did not act, however until after he'd heard the news bulletin at half past eleven which gave my description as one of the raiders. Still he did not call in the police. He could not be sure that he was on the right track, and he felt he might be making a fool of himself. But he called his men in from the hayfield, and taking the tractor just as it was, he set out to pay a visit to Elm Tree House. If he had found me in good health, and there had been a logical explanation forthcoming of the things that had been troubling him, then he would have made some excuse and departed. But coming down to the house he had almost collided with an ugly-looking stranger

168

driving a sports car, followed by Toby—who was supposed to be my boyfriend—in another car. Toby's arm had been round an unknown blonde, and this aroused Mr. Brent's suspicions further. Sid stopped his car, as did Toby. They yelled at Mr. Brent to back his tractor out of the way. Mr. Brent replied that in the first place he couldn't back a tractor and trailer all the way to the road, and in the second place, he intended to call on me, at Elm Tree House.

Rose lost her head. 'She's not there,' she cried.

'Where is she, then?' demanded Mr. Brent, and drove his tractor straight at Sid. Sid panicked and backed into Toby, who had no option but to back in his turn. And so it was that they had been brought back to the house.

We handcuffed Toby and Sid together and locked them into the back of the Security Van until the police came. Rose had hysterics, so we gave her some of the sloe gin; she was feeling the effects of it when the police arrived, but perhaps that was all for the best. I felt a little sorry for Rose.

*   *   *

We stood on the steps of the police station and argued. My father and mother were quarrelling about whether he should take me back to London straight away, or whether

I should go back home with her. I didn't particularly want to go with either of them, but I was too tired to argue. Hob—no, James Denison—stood beside me, taking it all in and not saying anything; the doctor said he wouldn't have his voice back for some time to come. He'd got his own clothes back, though, and was wearing a black sweater over grey slacks; he was waiting for the police to bring round his car, which they had towed away after the 'accident' on the river bank.

'You can see the child is worn out,' said my mother. 'She must come home. I'll get someone to clear out Elm Tree House later on.'

My father fancied a trip to the Metropolis for himself. 'She's perfectly all right,' he said testily. 'I'll drive her to London, she can collect her passport and some proper clothes and be off on her holiday abroad. That should set her up again.'

I thought about clothes. I was back in jeans and a sweater again; I would have liked Hob to have seen me in something more becoming. Or a nightdress. I flicked a glance at him and went back to studying my feet.

A police constable came out of the station and handed Hob some car keys, gesturing down the road to a white, four-door saloon. Hob nodded and smiled.

'You'll be off, then,' said my father to Hob, dismissing him. Neither of my parents seemed to think much of Hob, which annoyed me.

Hob nodded, without showing resentment. He pressed his hand to his stomach and flicked one enquiring eyebrow at me. I realised I was famished, too.

'Yes, I'd love to,' I said.

'What?' demanded my mother.

I translated for them. 'Hob says would we all like to have something to eat with him.'

'What?' repeated my father. 'I'll feed you on the way back to London.'

I was embarrassed for my family. I gave Hob a resigned apology of a shrug. That was that! I thought.

I could see Hob decide to give up. He lifted his hand to my parents in farewell, and went down the steps and along the street, where his car had been parked for him. I watched him, wishing that I knew how to behave with men. He started up the car and brought it to the foot of the steps. He opened the passenger door, but kept the engine running.

'Well, I'll be going,' I said to my parents. 'Hob's giving me a lift.'

'What . . . !'

'Where . . . ?'

I ran down the steps and got into the car beside Hob. My father and mother followed.

'Sarah!'

'What's got into you? Where are you going?'

I didn't know. 'Where do you live, Hob?

London?' He nodded and mouthed something.

'The police will have his address.' I told my parents. 'I'll send you a postcard after my holiday.'

I wound up the window and settled back as Hob drove off. Maybe I was being stupid, and maybe not. Maybe I was a romantic young idiot, who fancied being driven off into the sunset by the hero on the back of his white charger . . . sorry, white car. I reached for the seat belt and fastened it. Hob was already wearing his. He had sandals over the bandages on his feet; the doctor had wanted to sweep Hob off to hospital, but he'd refused to go. I thought I'd better offer to drive in a little while.

I wondered exactly where Hob lived, and whether I'd like his place. I thought that if I didn't like it, it would be easier to get him to move than to find another man.

After all, look what I'd had to go through to get this one!